Anonymous

Mavericks

Short stories rounded up

Anonymous

Mavericks
Short stories rounded up

ISBN/EAN: 9783744751520

Printed in Europe, USA, Canada, Australia, Japan

Cover: Foto ©Andreas Hilbeck / pixelio.de

More available books at **www.hansebooks.com**

MAVERICKS

THE RECORDING SPOOK.

MAVERICKS

SHORT STORIES ROUNDED UP

by

PUCK'S AUTHORS

illustrated by

PUCK'S ARTISTS

PUCK

KEPPLER & SCHWARZMANN

NEW YORK

1892

CONTENTS

A MODERN HANS SACHS.

"'Dot atvice don'd got noddings wrong mit it.'"

A MODERN HANS SACHS.

IT WAS NOT Frederick Preble's fault that he fell in love with Amalie Knecht.

Providence, in its inscrutable wisdom, always makes a tenor in the image of man. Frederick was a tenor, and having been made according to the customary plans and specifications of Providence, he had eyes, ears and a heart.

The girl was there; he saw her. He could n't help seeing her unless he shut his eyes; and, of course, he never wished to do that.

He heard her, too. And with his musically trained ear he noted that her laugh was an ascending chromatic scale, ending on a peculiarly piquant G sharp.

So he fell in love with her. And I, for one, do not see how he could help it.

He saw her every day; for he lived in the same house as she did. To be sure, his apartment was just under the chimney, while her father and herself occupied the floor behind the front door.

But love laughs at four flights of stairs. Why, Frederick's heart, every time he heard her laugh, used

to fall down those four flights of stairs, bumpetty-bump,
to lie at her feet.   It was all covered with bruises of
love, that heart of Frederick's; and still it kept on beating away, for her, for her.

But Papa Knecht would not have it.   He was willing to admit that Frederick was a "nice" young man
and could sing; but he did not seem to be able
to sing for dollars.   Papa Knecht had lots of
dollars.   Some of them had been left to him
by Grandpapa Knecht, who came over
years and years ago; and the rest Papa
Knecht had got by planting Grandpapa
Knecht's harvest in good soil and tend-
ing it while it grew.

Papa Knecht loved music, like a good
German, and he liked to hear tenors
sing; but he did not like to have them
marry his daughter unless they got very
large salaries and plenty of free adver-
tising in the newspapers.   Frederick got
fifteen dollars a week for singing in the
chorus, and did not even have his name
in the programme.   Papa Knecht did not like that.

Hans Sachs said Papa Knecht was right.

His name was not Hans Sachs.   It was Jacob Spie-
gelheim; but that is not a pretty name, so we shall call
him Hans Sachs.   He was not a poet; but a cobbler,
and a right-good cobbler, too.   He cobbled in the basement of the house in which Amalie and Frederick lived,
and he knew what was going on.   For the matter of that,

he knew everything that was going on in the neighborhood; but we shall say nothing about that.

It was Hans Sachs who found out that there was to be a great prize singing contest in Wiehawken. It was he who found out that the manager of the Delicatessen Opera Company had announced that if the prize was won by a tenor, he would offer him a good engagement. It was he who finally induced Frederick to enter the contest; though it must not be denied that Amalie temporarily suppressed the laugh and added a few influential tears to Hans's arguments. And it was Hans Sachs who induced Papa Knecht to go with his daughter to the singing contest.

Hans Sachs shut up his shop and went, too.

It was a very great contest. First, a little weazened man, with yellow eyes and a goat's beard, took three-quarters of an hour to read the conditions in a voice which sounded like the squeak of a toy chicken.

No one heard the conditions; but that made no difference; the contest was just as fierce.

The first singer was a tenor with a voice like a superannuated flute, and he sang, "Let Me Like a Soldier Fall." He fell more like a raw oyster.

The next was a sub-cutaneous bass; he made your flesh creep. He sang "Ohé, Mama!" It was very touching. Then came a baritone, whose vocal chords had been transformed, by years of application to the flowing bowl, into a long-distance telephone, so that his voice sounded as if it came from Chicago. He sang "The Christmas Tree."

2

There were several more with voices that could not be classed — except, possibly, as glassware — and Hans Sachs began to be tired.

"Of somepotty don'd got dot prize putty soon," he said, "I vill hef to gone und god me ein shchooner."

"Wait a little," said Papa Knecht, whose dialect had been mellowed by being filtered through a previous generation.

The next singer was a baritone, and he knew his business. He sang "The Yeoman's Wedding Song" in a style that carried away the audience and the judges.

So, when poor Frederick came out next, and with his lovely tenor voice sang Mozart's "Violets," he made the assembly sad.

The judges gave the prize to the baritone; the opera manager went off in a huff;

Papa Knecht smiled a two-edged smile, tucked his daughter under his arm and went home; and Hans Sachs went and drank "drei shchooner."

The next morning, Frederick walked into Hans Sachs's shop and sat down in a corner, whence he gazed upon Hans with an expression more melancholy than that of an overripe melon left drying on the vine.

"Ach, Himmel!" sighed Sachs.

"Oh, dear!" sighed Frederick; "that was fine advice you gave me, Meister."

"Dot atvice don'd got noddings wrong mit it. Aber you vos ein jump."

"A what?"

"Ein jump — ein Esel.   Vat for you sings dot put-me-in-mein-grafe kind of ein song for!   Don'd you got no senses, at all?   Vot you oxpect?"

"It is a lovely song, Meister," said Frederick; "the first art-song ever written."

"Yah, yah, ich weiss — aber id vos too goot!   Vat for you trow away high art on dose tuffers?"

"I trust I am always true to my art."

"By chimineddy!   You 'd pedder bin drue to Amalie."

"Why, Meister, I am!"

"Nein!   You can'd bin drue to art and her, too. Of you vant dot gel, dot beaudiful, heafenly anchel, you must shtop singin' vor art und sing vor tollars."

"O Meister!   Must I do that?"

"You ped your sveet life!   Can you ein high C sing?"

"I can sing," replied Frederick, proudly, "a high C that will put the gas out."

"Den vat for you don'd do dot?"

"What, put the gas out?"

"Nein; nein! sing your high C."

"Where, and when?"

"Leaf dot to me; I fix dot."

Hans Sachs was as good as his word.   He went to a musical agent in Union Square, and told him he had discovered a tenor who could sing a tremendous high C. The musical agent sent for Frederick, heard him sing it, and promptly secured him an engagement to sing at a Sunday night concert.

Hans knew the announcement of a new tenor, with a high C attachment, would induce the manager of the Delicatessen Opera Company to attend the concert. But he could not induce Papa Knecht to go.

No; Papa Knecht had lost all interest in tenors. He was now looking for a nice, fast young society man, who was *blasé* and ready to settle down and to introduce a wife into his charmed circle. Hans Sachs shook his head. Amalie went to his shop and wept.

"O Meister!" she said, sobbing; "what has become of Frederick? I have n't seen him since the contest."

"He vas all righd," said Hans; "und he vas godding reatty to susprise eferypotty. I vas lookin' oud vor dot."

"O Meister!" she said, falling upon his neck; "you have been our true friend."

"Dere, dere," he said, pushing her away somewhat hastily; "don't do dot; you shpiles my gollar."

And as he did not have one on, that made Amalie smile through her tears, so that her face looked like the fairy scene coming out from behind the cloud-drop in the last act of a pantomime. Hans Sachs turned away and sighed as she left the shop.

On Sunday night, Hans dressed himself in his finest and went to the concert. No doubt it was an interesting entertainment.　No doubt the programme was, as the daily papers said, next morning, "long and varied." But Sachs could see only one announcement, which read thus:

6.　" Di quella pira" ("*Il Trovatore*")....VERDI.
SIGNOR FREDERICO PREBELLIO.
(*His First Appearance in America.*)

"Yah, yah," he said to himself; "dot ish righd. Now he vill ein gross sugcess make."

The eventful moment, big with fate, finally arrived.

Frederick had insisted on being allowed to preface the "Di quella pira" with the "Ah, si ben mio," passing from one to the other without a break.

That was for the critics.

The audience did not care much about the "Ah, si," but when the orchestra began the familiar two measures of introduction to the high C aria, there was a flutter of expectation.

Frederick dashed into the aria boldly. When the time for the high C came, he took it at the back of the stage and walked down to the foot-lights with it. He shook it as a dog shakes a rat, and when he retired, the audience screamed with delight.　They called him out and made him do it over — and again — and again — and a fourth time, before they would let him go.

"Dot 's nod art," said Hans Sachs, smiling; "dot 's peesness."

And then he went home,

The next morning, he, Frederick and Amalie, sat in his shop and read all the morning papers. With one accord they declared that Frederick had no art, that he had only one good note, (the high C,) and that he had achieved a phenomenal hit with the audience. Frederick was half wild with mortification. Amalie wept on Sachs's collarless neck. But Sachs said:

"Vat do you vand? Dot von node, dot high C, is goot vor hundreds of tollars efery veek. Vaid a bit."

They did wait. They waited two days, and no offers came for Frederick. Sachs was troubled. He declared that the managers were holding off for fear they would have to give too high a salary. Finally he advised Frederick to call on the Delicatessen manager.

He did so.

The manager wanted him badly, but he pretended he did n't. He would not make an offer, though he said he would be willing to engage Frederick at a reasonable salary.

In despair the young tenor arose and left the office, saying:

"I won't take a cent less than seventy-five dollars a night. I 'm worth that or nothing."

When he went home, he kept away from Sachs. He saw Amalie and told her all.

"And now, my own dear little girl," he said; "there is but one road for us to happiness."

After that, their conversation fell into a whisper. They whispered upstairs and down, and Sachs saw them.

"Dere vas some mischiefs prewing." he said to

himself. "Dot poy don'd come near me, und now dey vispers. Vell, I ped you I keeps mine eyes oben."

That night, hiding in his shop, he heard the front door open and close very softly, and the next moment voices murmuring in front of his basement window. Then he threw open the shutter, and a stream of light shot out and illumined the figures of Frederick and Amalie, each carrying a small satchel. Hans Sachs was in the street in an instant.

"Nein; nein!" he said; "you vos going do elobe. Dot von'd do."

"We must. There is no other way left," said Frederick.

"O Meister!" sobbed Amalie, trying to fall on his neck; but he would n't let her.

"You must shtay!" he exclaimed.

And then he began to sing at the top of his lungs. Papa Knecht put his head out of the window and shouted:

"Stop that noise!"

Hans seized Amalie, and ran into the shop with her.

"Upshtairs mit you, gvick! Before you fadder vinds out!" he exclaimed.

That ended the elopement. The next morning Frederick got a letter from the manager, agreeing to engage him at seventy-five dollars a night, to sing three times a night. He took the letter at once to Papa Knecht, who embraced him and said:

"I always liked you, Freddy. Let me see you kiss her."

Then they all went down to see Hans Sachs, who

was so delighted he tried to drive pegs butt end first.
A'malie fell upon his neck successfully, once more laughing her sweet chromatic laugh, and then went off into
a corner with Frederick. Papa Knecht shook Sachs's
hand, and said:

"You have been a good friend. But tell me why
you have taken so much interest in this matter?"

Hans Sachs laid down his hammer, blew his nose,
and then looked up with his blue eyes swimming in
moisture.

"Vell," he said, in a trembling whisper; "I lofe
dot gel minezelf."

W. J. Henderson.

CHESTERFIELD'S POSTAL-CARDS

TO HIS SON.

Master A, Lincoln Chesterfield
Military & Classical Institute
Tarrytown
N.Y.

The address on all the postal-cards was the same.

It was as above.

CHESTERFIELD'S POSTAL-CARDS
TO HIS SON.

*The first postal-card contained the
following message.*

N. Y., 3/1/80.

My Dear Boy:

You are big enough to go to meeting barefoot, as
the Yankee captain said to me in '55 when I ran away
to sea, no older than you are now. I expect you to hoe
your own row, as I'm off by the 10:30 Pacific express.
I've no time for long letters, but I'll drop you a postal-
card of advice now and then. Rule No. 1: Tell the
truth. Rule No. 2: Show the sand that's in you.
Verbum sap-head, as the foreman used to say when I
ran a country weekly in '68.

Your aff'te Father,

J. Quincy A. Chesterfield.

The second postal-card:

LEADVILLE, COL., 17/1/80.

Dear Boy:

It's as cold here as the north end of a gravestone. I'm glad you're getting a good grip on the classics. Latin is useful: get the inside track and give the mare the head, as I heard the sports say in Cal., when I was lecturing in '75 on "Rum and Reform." Don't be scared of Greek either — especially as you have n't begun it yet. Rule 3: Never borrow trouble: it's no good crossing a river before you get there.

Your affectionate Father.

P. S. — The mine is doing A 1.

The third postal-card:

CHICAGO, 3/2/80.

Dear Boy:

Sorry to hear you fought that Smith — a little bit of a cuss. looking like a bar of soap after a hard day's wash. I knew his father in '69. when I was in the Conn. legislature. He's a pretty poor shoat, as we used to say in Cinn. in '60. when I was a telegraph clerk. Let the fellow alone. Rule 4: Keep out of a row, if you can. Rule 5: If you can't keep out, go in headfirst and fight like a fire-zouave. It's the first fight that prevents more; just as we used to nail the skin of a chipmunk to the barn to warn off the rest.

Y'r Father.

The fourth postal-card:

Dear Boy: OMAHA, 18/2/80.

A difference of opinion makes horse-races, as I've heard many a time in Ky., when I was a walking gent. on the southern circuit, in '58. But now you've whaled the Smith boy, go easy. The mine gets better and better.

Your Father.

The fifth postal-card:

ON PALACE CAR " DAKOTA,"
ILL. C. C. Ry, 29/2/80.

D'r Boy:

The mine is splendid. Over two millions in sight; and your revered dad owns a whole and undivided 1/5. Of course, I'll send you the $10. Rule No. 6: Pay C. O. D. always. I was clerk for an auctioneer in '57, and I saw that if a man don't pay on the nail, he soon gets sold out under the hammer. Tell the principal to draw on me for amt. due for schooling.

Y'r Father.

The sixth postal-card:

S. F., 21/3/80.

D'r Boy:

Yours rec'd. I taught school myself in '66, and I found all the boys knew more than I did. Rule 7: Don't think too much of yourself. The sun would shine, even if the cock did n't crow.

J. Quincy A. Chesterfield.

The seventh postal-card:

Dear Abe: LEADVILLE, 29/3/80.

Stick to the French grammar; it is n't easy. When I studied it in the trenches before Richmond in '64 the irregular verbs nearly threw me, but I mounted them every day as regularly as I did guard — though I did n't hone for it, as Johnny Reb used to say. What should I have done in Europe in '76, when I was introducing Cal. wines, if I 'd not known French? Rule 8: Learn all the foreign tongues you can. Rule 9: Learn to hold your own.

Y'r aff. Father.

The eighth postal-card:

                                    CHICAGO, 30/4/80.
D'r Boy:

I 've had no time to write. I 've gone into big spec with a man I first met in '65 when I took photos in Boston. They call Boston a good place to hail from: he and I got out of it quick, so as to hail from it as soon as possible. How do you get on with your mathematics?

Your Father,

J. Quincy A. Chesterfield.

The ninth postal-card:

Dear Abe: ST. LOUIS, 10 5 80.

I am sorry the arithmetic teacher is going to leave. I hope your next one will be as good. As I found in

'59 when I was a surveyor, it's a handy thing to have figures at the ends of your fingers. The spec looks bigger still. We've taken in the man who edited the N. Y. daily on which I was a reporter in '67.

Y'r affectionate Father.

The tenth postal-card

LEADVILLE, 20/5/80.

D'r Boy:

The mine is paying big money and I'm putting it all in the spec — for a permanent investment, as Uncle Dan'l said when I was on the Street in '72, before the panic made me sell my seat in the board. I've struck a streak of luck sure. Rule 10: When in luck, crowd things.

J. Quincy A. Chesterfield.

The eleventh postal-card:

LEADVILLE, 13/6/80.

My Dear Abe:

Mine looks badly; spec looks worse. But I don't give in; I've Yankee grit. I believe if a Yankee was lying at the point of death, he'd whittle it off to pick his teeth with. But I'm worried and hurried. Tell the principal I'll remit the quarter now due in a week or two.

J. Q. A. C.

The twelfth postal-card:

N. Y., 20/6/80.

My dear Boy:

The spec has caved in and all that's left of that whole and undivided 1/5 of mine has gone to pay the loss. Y'r father is as badly off as he was in '65 when he peddled a History of the Rebellion, or in '73 when he went to Fla. to manage an orange plantation. I must have time to look around. Telegraph me at once if the principal has not a teacher of mathematics yet. I'll apply for the place. I shall be glad to be with you again, my Abe.

Your affectionate Father.

The thirteenth postal-card:

GRAND CENTRAL DEPOT, N. Y., 21/6/80.

D'r Boy:

Y'r telegram rec'd. Can't accept place. Have sent ck. for quarter due. Leave 3:45 for China to introduce American inventions. Will write fully on P. M. steamer. Shall be back in 8 or 10 mo's — unless I run down to Australia. I think there's a spec in patent medicines down there.

Bless you, my boy.

Y'r Father,

J. Quincy A. Chesterfield.

Certificate.

———

I hereby certify that I have examined the postal-cards printed above, and that they are true and exact copies of the originals now in my possession.

J. Brander Matthews,

Notary Private.

New York, N. Y.,
July 1st, 1880.

MISTHER HANDHRIGAN'S LOVE STORY.

" ' Fine day, Misther Handhrigan,' sez she."

MISTHER HANDHRIGAN'S LOVE STORY.

"A QUARREL WITH yer swateheart is it, me b'y? Sure
an' that 's the lightest thrubble ye cud hev, but
it weighs the hivviest. Weemin is sthrange cattle; an'
the longer ye know thim, the sthranger ye 'll find thim.

"Maizie an' me hes been marrit this fifteen years
back; and sometimes I do be thinkin' it 's a new Maizie
I 'm makin' the acquentance av, ivery day. But, faith,
anny wan av the ould wans was good enough fer me!

"Did we quarrel, is it, me and Maizie, whin we
were coortin'? Did we do annythin' else till the ring
wint an her finger? An' it was nick an' go, but I lost
her altogither the last time we fell out.

"Ye see, I was wantin' me fling before I 'd settle
down with Maizie. I hed a loose foot, an' a fella for it;
an' there was n't a dance or a weddin' but I tuk the flure
an' me pick an' ch'ice av gairls.

"For a while it wint well enough, an' Maizie's huffs
an' sulks was pepper to the petaties — I was that sure
av her, d' ye mind? But whin Long Casey begin to
walk home from chapel with her, an' she wud n't look on
the same side o' the road I was an ————

"An' that was n't bad enough till he began to
stravague about the lane she lived in; an' one night I
seen her on the bank av the river with him; an' whin
she left him she hurried past me in the moonlight, runnin' like a fairy whin I spoke to her — Maizie, runnin'
away from ME!

'Afther that, for weeks, I cud n't get a word with
her. She niver kem out alone, an' her mother an' the
childer was always about her in the house, an' she sint
back the letthers I wrut her, 'ithout breakin' the wafer.
An' by this time, gairls an' dancin' was little thrubble
to me. I was losin' me slape an' the taste o' me vittles,

an' me face was the color av a dab av whitewash an a dhirty wall.

"Casey was always hangin' about with her father an' brothers; an' his intintions was well known to all, an' well approved av. An if it was n't for the widda mother he had, me own mother's crony, an' the dacintest soul in the parish, I 'd ha' bate him black an' blue, fer pre-shoomin' the way he did.

"Well, to-mek a long story short, one fine marnin' I whistled up me courage an' skirted away over the back fields to Maizie's house. The flowers was bloomin', I remimber, an' the big rosies was out; but I thought it sthrange to see no sowl about the place.

"I wint up to the dure an' lucked in, an' there was Maizie sittin' with her little sisther an her knee, combin' an' curlin' the child's white hair about her finger.

"I was thet hoongry for the sight av her, thet I stud gapin' like a fool.

"'The top o' the marnin' to ye, Miss Gar-r-r-vey,'" sez I, whin I got holt av me tongue, an' mekin' me v'ice up as bold as I cud.

"'Fine day, Misther Handhrigan,' sez she, with as much imperence as if I was comin' to vaccinet the family. 'Me father an' me brothers is down at the bog below,' sez she.

"'An' good weather they hev,' sez I.

"'An' me mother,' sez she, 'is away at Dhrimste-vellin,' sez she, 'to sell the butther.'

"But be this time I was in, an' luckin' about me for a stool to sit on.

"'I'm glad to hear it, Maizie,' sez I, 'for I'm comin' to see *you*.'

"'Oh, ye can hev no business with *me*, Misther Handhrigan,' sez she, curlin' her purty nose; 'no business, I am sure, sir, whativer, with me.'

"'Ye 're wrong there,' sez I; 'it's business, an' important business I hev; an' I can't spake before the child,' sez I.

"'Sure an' ye can,' sez she; 'what does the child know about business?'

"'I can't spake before the child on *my* business,' sez I, mighty detarmined; 'sind her into the gar-r-rden to pick a posy.'

"'I'll do nothin' av the kind,' sez she, tossing her head. 'Posy, indeed! It's well ye desarve one! Spake or lave it alone,' sez she. 'Wait yet, Dalia, love; Maizie 'll soon be done.'

"'Mebbe the posies is a-savin' fer Long Casey,' sez I, ragin', but quiet-like.

"'Mebbe they are,' sez she; 'at anny rate, he'd not be sindin' the child to pick thim.'

"'No; yersilf wud sind her fast enough, thin,' sez I.

"'Is that the business ye kem to spake about, Misther Handhrigan?' sez she, flushin' like wildfire, an' bitin' her lips.

"'It's par-r-rt av it,' sez I; 'an' more is, that from this time forrit I'll put no thrust in weemin.'

"'Poor things! What 'll become av thim?' sez she.

"'Scoff, if ye like,' sez I; 'but there's twinty gairls I might 'a' had for the askin'—

"'The craytures!' sez she, burstin' out with a laugh. 'Sure, an' ye 're not a Turk entirely,' sez she.

"'But I 've l'arned wan lesson,' sez I —

"'Only wan?' sez she. 'That 's a poor state of ignorance, is n't it, Dalia, dear?'

"'But it 'll last me me life-time,' sez I.

"'It wud nade to,' says she. 'Aisy, now, me lambie; ye 'll see the purty curls, how nice they 'll look.'

"'I 'm goin' to Ameriky, the day afther to-morrow,' sez I, coinin' the biggest lie I cud think av, an' watchin' her face, expectin' to see the big tear in a minute; for that was always the way with her, a laugh an' a cry in the one breath — but, faith, I did n't know me gairl.

"'Turn yer head a bit, Dalia,' sez she, combin' an' twistin' away at the ringlets. 'Sure an' that 'll be a nice jaunt for ye, Misther Handhrigan,' says she.

"'I 'm goin' with a lonely wretched har-r-rt, if that 'll make it a nice jaunt, Maizie,' sez I.

"'Why, but ye 'll take wan av thim gairls ye were mintionin'? sez she.

"'I might do worse,' sez I.

"'Sure an' ye might,' sez she, tyin' a bit av ribbon round the child's head, an' niver turnin' to luck at me.

"'Well, I 'll be sayin' good-by to ye, Miss Gar-r-r-vey,' sez I, takin' me hat up aff the flure.

"'Good-by an' good luck to ye,' sez she, as cool an' civil as the bailiff comin' to luck for the May Day rint.

"'An' ye 'll tell thim I 'm crossin' the ocean,' sez I, gittin' me stick out o' the carner; an', faith, I felt as if the lie I was tellin' was hardenin' into a truth, for I

knew Oirlan' wud niver hould me, once I said good-by
to Maizie.

"'I will, indade,' sez she, pelite an' plisint, but
niver afferin' to shake hands with me.

"'Well, good-by,' sez I, again.

"'Good-by, sir,' sez she, luckin' at me, this time,
with her big shinin' blue eyes, an' sorra the
hint av a tear to be seen.

"Ah, me b'y, whin I see Maizie's eyes
luckin' at me like that, I thought
I was done for, sure enough! Me
own tears was beginnin' to choke
me, so I turned about, an' walked
away, across the flure; but jest as
I raiched the dure, ready to step
out —

"'Dalia,' sez she, 'roon into
the gar-r-rden, an' pick a posy
for Misther Handhrigan.'

"But, faith, whin the child kem back, it was little I
cared for posies."

Madeline S. Bridges.

' OLD JONESY.

"We waited in solemn silence until it was pronounced safe to go on."

OLD JONESY.

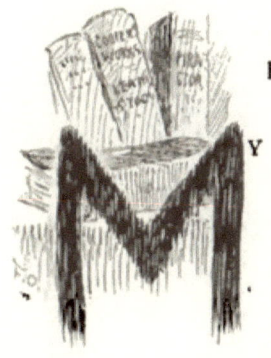Y ACQUAINTANCE with Old Jonesy
began with my school life. As I
was the first, and for several years
the only child of my parents, I was
believed in my early youth to be
altogether too valuable and fragile
to be endangered by contact with
the rougher and more common material at a public
school. Therefore, until I was about ten years old,
my education was carefully administered under strictly
home rule.

By the time that I was ten years old the advent of
other children had injured my uniqueness, and my
parents' faith in my value and fragility. I was accord-
ingly taken to a public school, with an education that
differed exceedingly from that of the average small boy
of my years, being in some respects superior and in
some inferior.

As its inferiority was in lines most valued by youth
of my age, to wit, a thorough acquaintance with well-
known games and received traditions, and its superiority
was mainly in arithmetic, geography and English
literature, which at that time did n't seem to count
for much, I was made to feel that I was somewhat
behind my fellows.

My father enlivened the walk to the school-house
by a number of very encouraging statements which had
rather a forced sound to me. He seemed to me to have
quite the air of a doctor giving to his patient the most
favorable prognosis possible of a very grave disease.
I walked up to the school-house with very much the
same sinking at heart that I had experienced on several
visits to the dentist; and, so strong was the power of
association, that I seemed to detect a faint odor of ether
in the air.

The school-mistress was a rather masculine-looking
person, with very black eyes and a very firm mouth.

She smiled on me in a way that was meant to be reassuring; but I interpreted her smile as signifying her delight on welcoming a new victim. As soon as my father left me, the school-mistress took me by the hand and led me to my desk. Then it was that I met Old Jonesy, though I did not at that time know him by his distinguishing appellation.

" This is Master William Jones," was what she said as she seated me by the side of a small boy of about my own age, with a light and freckled complexion, a mop of sandy hair, two extremely large front teeth, and a very sober face.

I was at that time too bewildered to be struck by the look of superior wisdom which I afterward recognized as the characteristic expression of Master William Jones. He eyed me all over in a very solemn way.

From my Oxford ties to my butterfly neck-tie, Master Jones subjected me to a careful and rigid scrutiny. He offered no opinion as the result of his examination; but after a few minutes he bent toward me and gravely whispered: " Got a knife ? "

I nodded, and he relapsed into silence and the contemplation of a soiled arithmetic which he held in his hand.

In considering the character of Old Jonesy, I am somewhat biased now by impressions of him that belong to my early youth. If in my reminiscences I present him as something of a fraud, I want it to be understood that he produced no such impression at that time, but was revered and looked up to with an unquestioning faith.

It was at recess, that brief oasis in the desert of school life which cheers and refreshes the weary seeker after knowledge, that I first learned in what estimation Old Jonesy was held by his fellow-students, and what my privilege was in being granted a seat by his side — a distinction which I was supposed to owe to the fact that my father was a committee-man. On the strength of a two-bladed knife which I produced, I was immediately made a member of Old Jonesy's celebrated band of Indian scouts.

In looking back upon Old Jonesy I can see that he must have been something of a reader, and that his inventions probably took color from the last story which he had read. At this period of my acquaintance with him he must, I think, have been reading Cooper's "Leather - Stocking Tales." He was regarded by the entire school as an expert hunter and guide, and he was the head and chief of a band of Indian scouts. Before

assigning me a position in this band of savages, Old
Jonesy examined my knife with great care. He said that
it would do, but suggested several improvements which
would make it more valuable as a scalping-knife. I was
disappointed to find that none of them seemed quite
practicable. To determine the acuteness of my sense of
smell, for the band of scouts tracked their prey largely
by scent, Old Jonesy made me shut my eyes, and then
held in succession one or two parcels under my nose.

I recognized one of them as sassafras, and, upon
saying so, was informed that the correct Indian pronunciation was "saxafrax." The others I failed on; but,
although the examination was not a complete success, I
was enrolled into the band as the "Black Eagle," by
which name I was to be known on the war-path.

On Saturday afternoons we used to go to a spot in
the woods which was known as "The Cave." There
certainly used to be a cave there, though I could find
nothing but an overhanging rock when I strolled up
there the other day; and as for the subterranean passage,
that only the boldest of the Indians dared to explore,
I could reach my cane through it from end to the other.
Everything in the woods seems to have shrunk since
those days. It was a wild and presumably dangerous
locality then, and it was only implicit confidence in the
skill and bravery of our leader that gave us courage to
explore the mysterious depths of the forest. Before
crossing the pasture lot which led to the woods, Old
Jonesy would lie down and put his ear to the ground.
If there had been a hostile band or a treacherous pale-

face within a radius of five miles, Old Jonesy's quick ear would have instantly detected it. We waited in solemn silence until it was pronounced safe to go on. Then, when the edge of the woods was reached, the twigs and bushes had to be very carefully examined.

Occasionally Old Jonesy would show us a broken twig, which indicated that about four hours before a deer had passed that way; or a torn leaf by which he could read that, in the early morning a pale-face, carrying a gun and wearing high boots and a broad felt hat, had pushed his way through the thicket. It was wonderful how much that boy could read from a broken twig. We spent the afternoon in hunting the enemy. When Old Jonesy's remarkable wood-lore and his powers of divination are considered, it is strange that the enemy should have succeeded in eluding us; but he did, and during the few weeks that the band of Indian scouts existed, we never found him, though we sought him faithfully.

After a few weeks of scouting, Old Jonesy must have finished Cooper and taken Charles Lever in hand; for we found, without any warning, that we were no longer a band of Indians, but officers in an Irish regiment.

We should have had horses to have enabled us to fill the parts that were now assigned to us; instead of which we were obliged to content ourselves with tales which Old Jonesy told us of his own feats of horseman-ship. They were certainly very impressive. As a vast amount of duelling was expected of us in this new rôle, Old Jonesy taught us to fence. Our swords were made of lath, the handles whittled down and a cross-piece

nailed on for a guard. Old Jonesy managed the duels.
He told us when we had been insulted; we could never
have found it out for ourselves. When the notice was
served that an insult had been offered, the principals
stalked off in a dignified silence while the seconds arranged the meeting.

The preliminaries having been settled to everybody's
satisfaction, at the solemn moment the principals were
escorted by their seconds to the appointed place. This
was usually behind the wood-shed in my father's yard.
On the ground, the swords were carefully inspected by the
seconds and measured to see that neither of the combat-
ants had any unfair advantage in the length. Jackets
were thrown off, and a leather belt drawn tightly around
the waist of each of the pale, determined warriors. Then
Old Jonesy said "en gardy," and the conflict began.

On the strength of a small mahogany box which I
found somewhere about the house, and which contained
originally some silver spoons, I was appointed the surgeon of the regiment, and I attended all of these
conflicts with the small box under my arm. My services
were only required once. Major Palmer, in a fierce
conflict, had a piece of skin knocked off the back of his
hand. He was supported in the arms of Old Jonesy
until I had treated the wound with court-plaster, ban-
daged his hand, and put his arm in a sling.

Then Old Jonesy began Marryat, and the wood-
shed was metamorphosed into a full-rigged ship, with
Old Jonesy as rear-admiral; and nothing but his coolness
and perfect seamanship could have brought us safely

" ' Boarders, follow me ! ' "

through some of the tempests we braved. It was a
thrilling sight to see him, standing on the two planks
across a wheel-barrow, which constituted our quarter-
deck, shouting orders to his crew through a section of
stove-pipe; and with what desperate daring did he lay
us along-side of a French three-decker, greatly our
superior in armament and tonnage; and, having thrown
grappling-irons over her side, lead his crew, with the
cry: "Boarders, follow me!" to her decks and victory.
The nautical terms with which he sprinked his conversation were simply astonishing. He knew knots and
splices without number. One particularly complicated
knot, which he called the "Pirates' Noose," was a secret
of his own.

At last Old Jonesy moved away, and his band of
followers gradually broke up. We did n't know where
he went to. Before his departure he hinted mysteriously
that he was about to engage in some perilous enterprise
which was likely to try even his iron nerve. He was
seen by some of us, riding down to the railway station
with his father and mother, and that was the last we
knew of him. A small boy who went to Troy on a visit
to some of his relatives, spread a report that he had
seen Old Jonesy there. He also saw a torch-light procession in Troy, and I think that he must have got a
little mixed up about it, for we gathered from the cross-
examinations to which we subjected him, the impression
that it had been a celebration in honor of Old Jonesy,
who rode on a black horse at the head of the procession.

It was a long time before the vivid impression of

Old Jonesy's skill and daring faded from my mind.
I believed in him thoroughly, as, indeed, we all did, and
I used to be in constant expectation that he would turn
up as the hero of some courageous exploit. It was
impossible that he should remain unknown and unhon-
ored. I should never have been surprised to have read
that the young man who, at the peril of his own life,
saved two women and four small children from the
burning building was named William Jones, or that
William Jones was named as a prominent candidate for
the Presidential chair.

Last Summer I slung my knapsack over my shoulder, and started for a walk through the upper part of
the county, off from the line of travel and the railroad,
through a broad village street where Lafayette and his
army once encamped, and by the white house where
Washington used to consult with Brother Jonathan, to
put up for a night at a tavern which had been on the
post-road, and where the fast stage had stopped while its
passengers supped in the long dining-room that now
echoed to the tread of the solitary maid who brought
me a beefsteak that, in spite of my remonstrances, had
been fried.

One glorious morning I had climbed a long hill,
and stopped for a minute on the top to rest and look
about me. Before me was a cross-road, and on the
corner a small country store; down the road were a few
straggling houses, and on one side a severely plain, low,
white building which I recognized as the school-house.
It had been long enough since I breakfasted to make the

prospect of crackers and cheese rather alluring, and I strolled leisurely toward the store.

The proprietor, a stout good-natured looking man with sandy hair, stood in his shirt-sleeves at the door. There was something strangely familiar about his face. I bade him good morning, and ate my crackers and cheese, while he looked me over curiously. Walking for pleasure is a problem that the rustic mind struggles with in vain. He questioned me a little about my walk, and when I had finished my lunch I bade him good

morning, and went on down the road, still puzzled by the familiarity of his face.

As I passed the school-house, the scholars were coming out for recess, and a small tow-headed boy with a freckled face stepped into the road before me, followed

by two or three others.   There was absolutely no mis-
taking that boy, and I looked down involuntarily to see
if I were wearing a jacket again, and had drifted back
in life thirty years.   The tow-headed boy and his followers carried in their hands sharp-pointed sticks, and I
heard him say: "You must creep up soft and spear 'em
when you see their backs."

I stopped them, and asked what they were going
to do.

"Spear salmon at the Falls," said the tow-headed
boy.

"What is your name?" I asked.

"William Jones," he answered.

"And is that your father's store?" I asked, point-
ing back down the road.

He turned and looked where I could still see the
proprietor standing in the door, with his hands in his
pockets, and nodded his head.

Then I knew that I had met Old Jonesy.

Walter Learned.

THE ROMANCE OF A SPOTTED MAN.

THE ROMANCE OF A SPOTTED MAN.

I AM THE ORIGINAL SPOTTED MAN, and have been known to fame as "The Leopard," for a score of years. Aside from The Leopard, my stage name is Peleg Porter, and my real name is — but never mind. I am to give a short sketch of Peleg Porter's love affair, and his real name is immaterial. I do solemnly assure the skeptical, that spotted men are as susceptible of the tender passion as their more fortunate brethren, and their *affaires d'amour* are always romantic from the fact that leopard-men and other freaks must live, love and die in channels that run wide of the commonplace.

It happened that, during the Summer of '87, I entered into a two weeks' engagement to exhibit my spots in a Chicago museum, and I repaired thither to fulfill my contract. By one of those coincidences which hapless fortune is ever forcing upon us poor mortals, it also happened that Mademoiselle Irene Leroy, a snake-

charmer of national repute, began an engagement at
the same museum and at the same time with myself.

Irene was beautiful! Faultless of feature, she
united with her beauty a willowy movement of her
plump limbs that came insensibly from a constant hand-
ling of her serpents. The platform whereon she ex-
hibited her reptiles was next to mine; and many and
many a time have I wished myself an Indian cobra, that
I might embrace her with my shining coils, and receive
the little love-pats which her tiny hands bestowed upon
her pets; but, alas! I was only a poor man, whose
single fortune was his spots, and who could only look
upon Irene and vainly sigh.

How the fat man used to laugh at me! and the
Albino people, too, what fun they had at my expense!
But Love is a stranger to all scorn but his lady's, and I
continued to glance and sigh for the favor of fair Irene.

Pursuing these tactics, I finally managed to gain
the attention of my adored one. At first, she would
only vouchsafe me a glance; then I saw with delight
that she bestowed a kindly attention upon the brief
remarks anent myself, which I essayed when the showman called the attention of his audience to me. When
I bowed, thereafter, Irene was the cynosure of the
courtesy. From these little exchanges of good will we
came, at last, to smiles, and she would nod in a friendly
way when she ascended her platform in the morning for
the day's exhibition. Finally, one day of days, she
came over to my stage and brought a little snake to
show me. Emboldened by her glances, I patted the

young reptile, and courted his friendship because I
imagined to gain Irene's favor.

From that time until near the close of my engagement we were very intimate, and my heart came to be
assailed with the deepest love. Did she reciprocate my
affection? I fondly thought so; for, latterly, when I
turned in her direction, her eyes would droop toward the
blue box that held her serpents, and a blush would
mantle her cheek. "She loves me!" I rapturously
thought.

The fortnight of my engagement expired on Saturday night, and Friday, burning with a passion I could

not trust to speech, I indited a tender epistle, filled with
endearing expressions, and breathing the sentiments of
my love. I wrote how madly I loved her, how my whole
heart was wrapped in her beautiful being, and asked, in
conclusion, that she become my bride, give up the
museum business, and retire with me to the little Michigan farm, which twenty years of exhibiting to crowded
houses and a shrewd investment of the proceeds had
netted me. With trembling hands I folded the missive,
and sent it to her by a Zulu chief, who was my friend.

I will not watch her when she reads it, thought I,
for it might embarrass her. I will look away until she
pens me an answer.

So I watched the pianist as he thumped his patient
instrument, and fell into a sweet revery, which lasted
until my sable friend re-appeared and thrust my answer
into my hand. It was my letter. She had replied by
writing upon the back. I read the scrawl, and was
undone. Oh, heavens! Irene was a coquette. Here is
her reply:

peleg Portir
> *sur*
>> *when i git Marrid i want A feller all of One Color*
>>> *ireen*

Oh, the pity of it! The spots that had made my
fortune had finally wrecked my life. The rest of that
Friday was drear, indeed, and it passed like a dream of
purgatory. I could not realize that Irene had so sud-

denly and cruelly gone out of my life.   I read and re-
read her note; and, finally, when night came and I left
the museum for my lodgings, I sank into a slumber re-
plete with troubled dreams.

I could not give up Irene.   I arose on Saturday
morning, resolved to see her, and to request, from her
own lips, another answer ere we parted forever.

This Saturday was to be a great day at
the museum.   My Zulu friend was
to perform a war-dance in his
bare feet upon broken glass;

I was billed for a humorous
lecture, and Irene was to
perform with an immense
boa - constrictor "that had
never before been out of his
cage," (so the bills said, but
I found this to be a fabrica-
tion, pure and simple.)   I
trembled for Irene, but what
was she to me now? Nothing
more than a mere acquaintance.   Our two weeks of companionship were nearly finished.   When Saturday night
had passed, Irene would take her serpents to St. Paul;
and I, broken-hearted, would repair to my rural home
and pass my life in an endeavor to erase that cruel
coquette from mind and heart.

But was it all over?   I was fain to hope differently.

That Saturday morning when I arose and started for the museum, I felt as many another rejected lover, and I burned to perform some heroic act which would prove to Irene that, although I *was* a leopard-man, I could yet do and dare like a regular hero more fortunate epidermically. At any rate, I could seek her and tell my love with my own lips; she would not, she could not, deny me. Thinking thus, I ascended the museum stairs with more than my wonted dignity.

Shortly afterward, Irene came and walked directly past me to her stage, without even one glance in my direction. My heart sank within me, for, by this action, I was clearly given to understand that her ruthless note was the final blow to our intimacy. Henceforward we were to be strangers.

I was resolved that my despair should not be manifested, for I would have died rather than Irene should know I felt her disfavor so keenly. In the face of her stern demeanor, all thoughts of asking her to reconsider the refusal of my love vanished like dew in a morning sun. She would have none of me. Very good, thought I; I will show you, Ma'm'selle, that I can live without you!

I have never delivered so humorous a lecture as on that Saturday night. The audience screamed with mirth, the showman snickered, and every freak in the hall (save Irene) laughed immoderately. I answered numerous *encores*, and was finally permitted to make my bow and sit down. Irene was next on the programme, and I wondered if she would acquit herself as well as I had done.

Two men pushed through the crowd of spectators, lugging a large box, which they deposited upon the platform as carefully as though it had been filled with dynamite.   Irene stood up, grand, beautiful, intrepid.

"Ladies and gentlemen," said the lecturer, "you see before you, Mademoiselle Irene Leroy, the peerless Circassian queen and snake-charmer par-excellence of the old world.   Her fame is co-extensive with all Europe. She has appeared before kings and princes of the blood royal in her fearless acts, and has been applauded and decorated by some of the greatest rulers of the present age. By offering a fabulous sum, Messrs. Mudge & Fudge, the foremost spirits in the amusement world, secured Ma'm'selle Irene for a brief engagement, during which it was stipulated that she should give one, and only one performance with her mammoth boa-constrictor, Salvadore.   This reptile measures twenty-four feet in length, and it seems, indeed, as though it could be but certain death to venture in his power; yet so great is the lady's sway over the reptilian kingdom, that she will handle Salvadore with the greatest ease! Behold! the fearless Irene approaches and loosens the lid — she is at the mercy of the serpent!"

Irene, perfectly calm and collected, coaxed the snake from his box, and he glided out upon the floor. Then he wound himself in sinuous coils about her body, and she, lofty and erect, looked like a placid Hindoo god in the meshes of Ananta.

But, suddenly, she uttered a scream, and I saw the snake's coils tighten about her slender form.   She had lost control of Salvadore, and he was crushing her to death! The audience pressed fearfully back, and the showman threw up his hands wildly. I realized that my opportunity had arrived. Now was my time to convince Irene of my heroism and win her hand.

"Have courage, Irene," I cried; "I will save you!"

Seizing a long sword belonging to the Zulu chief, with one mad jump I sprang upon her platform, and, quicker than it takes to tell it, I had decapitated Salvadore, and laid him dead at my loved one's feet. Irene fainted and fell upon the stage. Before I could catch her in my arms, the showman grasped my shoulder.

"What did you do that for?" he cried, choking with anger. "That was a part of the act."

"I saved my darling's life," I said, drawing myself from his grasp, and stooping over the unconscious Irene.

"Saved her life, indeed!" he cried. "The snake was trained — it was that act that made her reputation — that was her *chef d'oeuvre*. Get off this stage, sir; go to your own platform!"

I rose to my feet, and the truth began to dawn upon me. The serpent had been trained to tighten his coils, Irene screamed, and the showman became terrified, just to give the audience a shock, and I, blockhead that I was! had been the victim of a mere piece of acting. How I got out of that hall and to my hotel, I do not know; but, ah! the long, long hours that I battled with my mortification and despair. What would Irene think of me now? What *could* she think? I could conceive but one answer to this question — my case had become utterly hopeless, if it had not been so before. I determined to leave Chicago at once, and to take the first train for Michigan.

As I was preparing for my journey, the call-boy knocked at my door, and presented me with a letter. From Mudge & Fudge, I thought, with my salary — but, no! O ye Angelic Fates! that letter was from Irene, and I read and kissed the misspelled text with frantic joy. What wonder that I should feel transported!

deer peleg

i dont care about the snaik i had had so menny lovers that was fikel that i thot you was fikel to my last lover was a Iron jawed man and he Deceeved me so i thot id see If you loved me Real and tru thats why i wrot you as i did to see if youd deceeved Me and would love me cnny more i dont care about the snaik i love you and if you Want me ill be yourn so no More from

ireen

Kind reader, need I say anything more? Need I

dwell upon the happiness of that reconciliation? I feel that further words are unnecessary. I hope you will find as much joy in wedded life as has the Spotted Man.

William Wallace Cook.

RECOLLECTIONS OF A BUSY LIFE.

"*Here I found that my labors were none the less exacting.*"

RECOLLECTIONS OF A BUSY LIFE.

Chapter I.

A FACT WHICH I have always regarded as in a measure foretokening my busy life is that I was born a few weeks after the Fourth of July, so that there have been comparatively few holidays for me. I was obliged to wait six months for my first Christmas, nearly a year for my first celebration of the day of Independence, and a full year for my first birthday.

In general, I am not a believer in portents; yet, when the holidays come around, and I am sitting at the Christmas banquet, I can not escape the feeling that I am eating last year's turkey, nor on the glorious Fourth can I break away from the conviction that I am listening to last year's orations.

But let us drop these vain speculations, and commence a tale of my busy life.

I have now completed my sixth year.

During my first twelve-month, finding no other employment at hand by which to gain my living, I determined to lay aside all considerations of dignity, and to engage in a course of unremitting grief. In this business I prospered beyond my hopes, and, showing how perseverance may find its reward even in the simplest vocation, I was at all times able to keep myself well and happy.

It may be well here to point out what I consider an error in the course pursued by other children. They are content to assuage their grief after crying until they have obtained everything they can think of. It was my own practice, however — and I now look back at this as presaging the tireless industry I have since shown — to cry not only until I had obtained everything I could think of, but to continue crying, letting other people think of things. They often thought of things that pleased me beyond measure.

Nor was there more than one occasion of importance when lamentation failed me. This was in the early part of my early Summer when, after the first hot days, there came about a terrifying commotion. The room in which I played was invaded by a frightful gloom; fitful light flashed at the windows; the wind rose; the glass was beaten against by rain and hail, and there were bursts of deafening noise such as I had never (to my recollection) heard. Wishing this immediately discontinued, I began to cry; but the commotion growing only more terrible, I abandoned this course, and hastily essayed to appease a power that I could not coerce. I performed the patty-cake, repeated in a sweet voice the three words that I knew, and enacted a smile.

I know now that it was a thunderstorm that I tried to cajole; and though I laugh at my simplicity, yet the incident shows, perhaps, some fertility of expedient.

At the end of the year, so good progress had I shown, so strong and fat had I become, that I was promoted to a seat at the family table. Here I found that my labors were none the less exacting, nor their reward the less gratifying. Within twelve months I had broken nearly a complete set of china, and had practically ruined a bale of table-cloths. Devoting myself to the great truths of science — for the study of which I can not recommend too early a date — I burned my hands 365 times on the coffee-urn, and an equal number of times on the tea-pot.

But it must not be supposed that I neglected the arts. Like every other person who tells about himself, I put myself in the way of learning everything. I invented hammered metal-work, and myself hammered two trays into artistic and shapeless masses.

Chapter II.

The studies in caloric and metallurgy which I have mentioned as occupying part of my second year were pursued in intervals of rest from other exercises in which the bent of my mind made me take but little interest.

My father and mother, whom at this time I looked upon as finished linguists, were accustomed to insist on

my attempting to pronounce words of a language other
than my own.   My mother was usually satisfied to rap-
ture when I rendered any combination of sounds into
"Ah — Bung!" but my father, who affected to possess
a most sensitive ear, would often deny me my ration of
milk (to spill on the table), or of rare beef (to drop to
the cat), until I had achieved a more detailed success.
He often ended his lessons by charging me to say
"rhinoceros," but he did this more
to confuse than to instruct me.

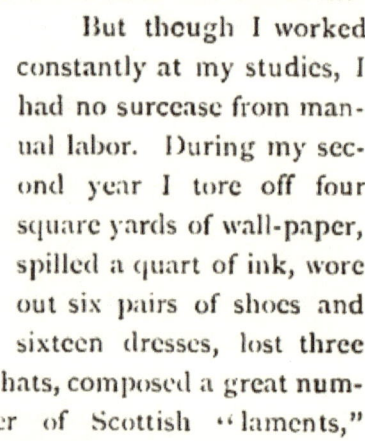

But though I worked
constantly at my studies, I
had no surcease from man-
ual labor. During my second year I tore off four
square yards of wall-paper,
spilled a quart of ink, wore
out six pairs of shoes and
sixteen dresses, lost three
hats, composed a great number of Scottish "laments,"
and put into the grate at odd
intervals (it will be remembered that I had only the
cold season to work in, and that a spy was kept upon
my actions by my unscrupulous parents) the following
property :

    1 thermometer, 1 shaving-brush, 4 papers of pins,
6 important letters, 2 sets playing blocks. 20 playing
cards, each card from a different pack. 1 jumping-jack
(old), 1 treatise on "How to Raise Children," 15 toys

(assorted), 2 quarts of water, and various matters from the desk of my father, a writer by profession, among these a MS. story, entitled, " Mr. Jimson's Baby," being a wonderfully humorous account of the doings of a certain infant. I burned this story with some other things (and some others) to show my father that his own child could not be outvied in delicate humor.

In ending this chapter, I will say that while I am by no means satisfied with these successes, they nevertheless brought me to higher and more varied activities.

Chapter III.

Until the age of two years, at which I had now arrived, my acquaintance had been limited to a class of people consisting of my parents and the nurse.

I will not claim that I had always the penetration to regard these people with disfavor, but my now advancing mental strength made this a natural step. I therefore, as occasion presented itself, abstracted myself from their company, and sought the society of the learned. My first experience of a wider life was afforded by trips that I took to a subterranean cavern beneath the house.

There existed a marvelous being (whom I now have occasion to suppose was our cook), and I basked in the rays of her Aspasian converse. It was from her that I obtained much of my information concerning " boogy " men. I also became acquainted in the true pronunciation of the Irish language, and well versed in the arts of cookery. Further (for I had ever a practical turn), I learned how to take cookies, cake and bread, off the table without detection, while things more indigestible than these the cook would herself choose out with wonderful skill, and present to me.

Among the unique and desirable possessions of the cook was a cat; and a little computation that I have made shows that I chased this cat more than two thousand miles. She fled over a regular route, which she came to know so well that she was always able to elude me, but which I came to know so well that never for more than an instant could she remain in one place.

From under the table she went under the stove, thence behind a basket, thence she jumped into a window-seat. She always made a peculiar sharp sound when I dislodged her from this retreat; and while I stood somewhat terrified, she took advantage to jump under the table again. But I knew that this position offered no harm, and the pursuit recommenced.

When the cat and I had encored each other's parts long enough to set the cook into a fit, she would open the door and drive the cat out. It was in the language of the soft North of Ireland that she ordered the cat to leave, and by fortune it was through this circumstance that I came more into favor with my father,

who was always anxious for my linguistic advancement;
for, though I still rendered very ill each word that he
gave me to pronounce, he was obliged to own to my
mother, when by chance he heard me say "Ashgo-roo"
to the cat, that I could imitate the Irish as well as he
could himself — if not better.

I have since heard him tell Irish dialect stories —
which he generally tells in Dutch or Hebrew — and I
can bear this statement out.

During this period my mind was growing apace.
At the age of two and one-half I became aware one day
that *I* hiccoughed. Previously I had had no idea *who*
hiccoughed. At first I tried to run away from it, but
finding this effort vain, I rapped smartly on my breast,
and commanded: "Top it!"

A second incident of this time will show that I continued my progress in science; for my father (who, as
he had once essayed to confuse my tongue, now often
tried to overwhelm my reason,) idly asking me one day
in the midst of a Minnesota Winter where the snow
came from, I immediately blew a Thor-like blast, and
answering, "Who-o-o wind," gave him a decided dis-
comfiture.

Chapter IV.

Having now arrived at the age of three, I was allowed to venture out of doors to join the children of
our neighbors, whom with wonder I had seen disporting
in strange but interesting games before our windows.

For a long time after I had joined them, these
little people were a mystery to me, and many a heart-

ache I experienced at my lack of success in fraternizing with them.

In order to make myself a welcome addition to their party, I took out with me (by stealth) my best toys. Whereupon they played express with my wagon without asking or allowing me to participate; they rode my velocipede, while I, all in good faith, made a laughing-stock of myself, by running breathless at their side; they whipped my top, and answered my expostulations by threats of whipping me. When they desired it, I traded my toys for theirs, and in these cases I had the unhappiness of my own dissatisfaction coupled with the mortification of being considered a ninny by my parents, who supposed that I made the trades on my judgement. When the children grew tired of my toys and my complaisance, they would go apart and play by themselves, ostentatiously affecting that while they found my society distasteful, they were fairly intoxicated with the company of one another. And when they were ready to quit sport for the day, they would start a game of hide-and-seek, and without question pitching upon me to blind, would leave me to look vainly for them after they had scattered giggling to their homes.

In the meantime I became a factor in the administration of our house. The cook, whom I still visited, had taken a habit (as I learned from the assertions of my father) of retaining the paper when it was delivered by the newsboy. Seeing her reading one evening, I suddenly demanded (after I had eaten to satiety of the new cookies) "That old pakur, new pakur?" "New!"

stammered the guilty creature. "Then give me and I give my papa, and 'top this monkey bidnit," I replied.

Nor with my other occupations did I neglect my investigations in philosophy. At luncheon one day, where I ate in great haste in order to keep an appointment with my tin soldiers, I took a drink of water. Its effects pleased me much, and drawing a long breath of satisfaction, I heralded to the family my neat discovery: "Ha-a! cold water make bread go down good."

As time advanced, becoming an equal party in the ventures of the children upon the street, I entered into their pursuits with all my natural industry. We ran our wagons hundreds of miles, learned architecture in the sand-piles, instituted systems of money and organized forces of police to cope with bands of robbers. With one exception all went well with me.

There was a desperado of six who terrorized our neighborhood, and offered constant menace to our peace, so that in the end my father felt obliged to report him to his parents; and this was so wise a step that for a week I hardly durst set foot outside our door.

This enemy was at last overthrown in a singular way. While making free and rough use one day of my wagon, he broke the box off and bent the axle. He knelt down to examine the latter, and I, coming up with the box and staggering under its heavy weight, stumbled against the wheel and brought the box down full upon his head. Instead of attacking me, he jumped up and ran away; and I found myself a hero while the desperado was jeered off the street.

Some conclusions of my long study of children may here not be amiss. Though fickle and tyrannical, they are far more agreeable in intercourse than men; for, while children have unlimited expedient of converse and amusement, men are entirely restricted to asking us a few stale questions, such as, "How old are you?" "What is your name?" "What are you going to be, my boy, when you are a man?" and to fetching us sly cracks, and then looking away with a pretence of playfulness; showing not only great paucity of ideas but a paltriness thereof truly depressing.

These memoirs of my busy life, which now draw to a close, I end with a feeling of sadness. If men dwell regretfully upon their youth, the memory of which they may at any time recall, it is natural that I should now linger fondly upon my childhood, the memories of which (as I know from older people) must soon be obscured and lost; nay, which I shall with mortification hear recalled when my parents fatuously tell my childish sayings. How shadowy soever it may grow, this period of life has been real to me; it has been made up of days coming and going, of gladness and grief, of silent expectancy of praise for little acts of merit and of hopes of pardon for little trespasses. I think of the constant labor that a little fellow must undertake to learn from dumb watching the meaning of smiles and of frowns, and then from these, what is thought good and what bad.

Other children will no doubt find, as I have, that in this strange world they must often descend to hypocrisies to win encomiums; that they must even, alas, conceal their real opinion of some traits of their parents. Yet children have such natures that they will find something in any parents to love and respect; and parents can not fail to see much to rouse affection in the worst of children.

I knew this last when much younger than I am now; for one day when, after having been freshly clad, I went out and played in the dirt, and my mother, obliged to renew my dress, rebuked me most earnestly, so that no merit appeared in my character, I nevertheless, as I have said, knew there was still something about me that fastened her affection, and interrupting her by throwing my arms around her neck, I said: "But you love me aucky hard allee same." And so it turned out she did. Good-by to you and to my little self.

Cameron Fish.
W. F.

THE WIGHT THAT QUAILED.

"*Running through hot gulf-streams*
of gore up to their eyes."

THE WIGHT THAT QUAILED.

By

GRUBHARD STRIPLING.

I.

THERE WAS a seashore, some guns, a girl gamin and a boy gamin.

These children were born without relations, were no relation to each other, and the woman who had them in charge led them a perfect dog's life — a sort of whipper-in. While beating them, she made them say so many prayers and psalms, that for diversion the boy took to lying, stealing and swearing. The girl took to sassing back.

To-day, both of them have run far away to the shore, and it is well she can not hear what the wild waifs are saying.

Nick had rifled from somewhere an old Winchester repeater. It was just the thing for firing off jokes on the British public. But the boy took no such aim.

Being unfortunate himself, he sought to make others suffer by drawing their pictures. To-day he only shoots off a few fingers. That makes Hasie cry. That pleases him. He laughs. To this Hasie objects so much, that Nick leaves off swearing long enough to kiss her. Then they go to walk with a volatile goat, named Ammonia. As they walk, the girl's long hair blows in Nick's eyes. It blinds the boy for a moment. It comes between him and all his *future aims.* Forever after that his sight is a little dimmed.

II.

Midway between Afric's soda fountains and the steppes of India Rubba, is a desert. Here the snail trains of the British Civil Service Relief Corps of the International Copyright Syndicate are always obliged to rest after a season of equatorial engagements.

Torkinow, the society reporter of *The Cape Town Tropics,* and the captain of this great caravan, is sitting upon a clump of cacti, making a pair of trousers out of two old ash-barrels.

An individual who had fallen in with him at a Sepoy dug-out, sat somewhat apart, drawing pictures on the sands of the desert.

"Say, Meissonier, come in out of the simoom, and bring the pictures with yer!" said Torkinow. But the artist did n't move.

"Show what you have on paper, and if I like 'em I'll make your fortune," the reporter persisted, being much taken with Nick's manners. Oh, by the way, this was Nick.

When he had finally taken a look at some cartoons, Torkinow said:

"Send 'em to *The Tropics*."

"Go there yourself!" said Nick, trying to throw dust in his eyes.

"Well, you 've got sand! Those gory battle daubs won't be worth a 'bob' when the War is over. Say, Verestchagin, going to open an art gallery in the Soudan?"

So the drawings were sent to illustrate Torkinow's fashion notes.

Just at dawn one night there was an unexpected attack by native Hoodoos on the *B. and S. Infantry* — mostly beardless boys. There was a surge of black bodies, a rush of hot sand, a splashing of Nile mud, and assegais a-flying through the air.

Swish! came a simitar where Nick swayed, grappling two Oriental Musclemen, while Torkinow, for once having nothing to say, was engaged in poking out his adversary's eyes. Nick threw a back hand-spring as that simitar came down, and grabbed Torkinow away by the hair, while he poured pistol shots around them, running through hot gulf-streams of gore up to their eyes. When he had reached a place of safety, Torkinow said that Nick had saved his life. For a time the artist was very wrong in the head. He would cry,

"See that Cartoon! They 're after me, after me! Cartoon, Cartoon!" Then, "Is n't that Hasie?"

III.

Stopping, on his way home to London, in many populous towns, Nick had spent all his time and money in hunting out disreputable characters, drinking them into delirium tremens, and, then, painting their portraits. He had a high, pure love for his Art.

After reaching London, he starved in great shape for some days, and then, very leisurely, he called for his monthly allowance, and afterward invited himself to a lunch of beefsteak and onions, corned beef and cabbage, with Torkinow.

Here Nick received a call from one of the proprietors of the *Tropics.* This man had come to ask for more pictures. But Nick had just seen some of his cartoons in a cigar-shop where a crowd of corner loafers had congregated, and the artist felt that he and Fame could henceforth travel tête-à-tête, dispensing with the party who had introduced them. He was very properly incensed at the man's desire to retain the originals of all his drawings; but Nick's brow-beating method of inducing him to return them, proved that his own late hairbreadth escape had made very little impression on the young man's naturally hard and insolent character.

After abusing thoroughly this gentleman, who was already afflicted with age, stoutness, respectability and heart-disease, this youth with the fine artistic temperament went out of doors to muse upon the pride and vain-glory, the hatred and malice of humanity and all the sordid aims of this little life of ours.

IV.

As Nick stood on the embankment, planning how he would one day set the Thames on fire, a lady stood within a few feet of him and a gray cloak; and the moment Nick saw her, he knew she was Hasie. Hasie was now about twenty; but she was still wearing the same cloak she wore at ten.

When Hasie saw Nick she nodded to him just as if next week was the day before yesterday. She said she was glad he was not dead, because she needed him to wash her paint-brushes.

So she, too, was an artist!

Ought he not to have recognized "the temperament" at her first word?

Hasie said she lived with a red-haired girl who was a Suppressionist.

Hasie's housekeeping was a good deal like her pictures — sketchy. When Nick went to see her he found that she subsisted principally upon crackers and chewing-gum; and he dreamed about the time when he should have the right to nurture her tenderly upon beefsteak and onions, corned beef and cabbage. At present, however, Hasie had only a palette for paint.

He must now struggle to answer her confiding appeals to his artistic taste, to explain to her why all her ideal heads invariably had a cast in one eye. The red-haired Suppressionist watched them silently, grinning and bearing it. She made faces and five o'clock tea that tasted of turpentine.

One day Nick came in and thrust his umbrella through Hasie's very latest. He said in a broken voice:

"Dear, you can't paint any more than a cat. Your pictures are chromos. Besides, who wants Ideals nowadays? Give up Ideals and try to live down to me. Let me daub for both. I've enough red paint to give gore for the millions who just dote on my horrors of war. The upper ten thousand prefer subjects with more polish about them — their own boots nicely varnished. But I would even black those for them now to get money. I am mercenary, dear, since I began to dream of Matrimony."

Up spoke the Suppressionist. "Paint a picture, each of you, called 'Matrimony,' making it tell the story of one who never told her love; but — "

"Ate crackers and chewing-gum," put in Nick. "I take the idea. Hasie, *catchy-vous-on*, as Krami says?"

V.

One day the two girls went over to France. The cross in her picture's eye had infected Hasie's temper. But Nick's picture had the crookedest look. His model herself perceived it. It was so like her, and it happened that she was so like everything hateful in woman that

for once she saw herself as others saw her, and loathed
herself and the artist who had so strangely chosen her
bad face to illustrate a noble theme.

Nick had meant this picture called " Matrimony "
to embody all his best ideas of the True and the Beautiful. But, alas! his life had made him more familiar
with many forms of Falsehood and Ugliness, and from
these his nature had never shrunk.

One evening, when the thermometer stood at
Fahrenheit, Hasie had her head out a window; when
suddenly a huge white horse stopped at Hasie's door.
The red-haired girl joined her friend at the window.
The man on the horse called out courteously:

" Ah, there, Hasie! Nick is blind."

Torkinow had come for her; so this girl, who was
selfish and cold, a soul tied to Ideals, never doubted for
a moment that it was her duty now to marry Nick out

of pity. She and the red-haired girl went to London and climbed up to Nick's studio. But before they greeted the artist, a soiled canvas claimed their attention.

"Why, it is half washed off!" cried Hasie; "and it is Nick's picture of 'Matrimony.' But no wonder his better angel made him destroy it, for it is terrible. It has some beauty; but it is bold and hard and defiant.

"If this is Nick's best, there can not be an atom of Sweetness and Light in his whole composition. He is blind, blind indeed! I can not marry a man unable to see beyond or above this fleshly thing. ·

"I quail before such a sacrifice.

"But you, my friend, can wed him. You could care for him enough to try to inspire him to better things. You pretend to be Hasie, and Nick being blind, will never know of the deception! I wish you joy of him. This wight has quailed."

Nick married the red-haired girl, and let her think she had fooled him. But he knew of the deception all the time, and made the Suppressionist a pretty hard husband.

There might have been a different ending to this story. But this is different enough. It is not a sentimental tale. It is only a natural one. This is an age of Realism.

Kate W. Rider.

BIDDY'S DREAM.

"Off I went and tould Father Pether the whole business."

BIDDY'S DREAM.

MY WIFE, BIDDY O'DWYER, is the quietest, da-
centest crathur in this world. The work she
can do and her industhry bates creation,
and she 's asy kept up, too, for its very little she ates, and drinks nothin' at all.

She has a fine cowld hand for the but-
ther, which same guided and directed me in my choice
the day I towld ould O'Dwyer I 'd take his Biddy with
ten pounds down, the ould bay mare, and my pick of his
runners, and if he 'd give me two out of them, I 'd ax
no fat pig, for there was n't a man in Ireland, let alone
Connaught, that had purtier fat pigs than Mike O'Dwyer.

"Aye! Mike," says I, "I 'll take your Biddy," says
I, "before and forninst Jane or Kitty Duff, who are
posted up on the chapel for fifty pounds a-piece, and two
three-year-old heifers; and more by token," says I, "I 'll
give her such a haulin' home as what Queen Victoria herself might be proud of, and the Miss Duffs 'ill be in it
too, to dance their quadrilles and their boarding-school
airs, while Biddy and I will tune up a good ould Irish jig,
which I always towld ould Lynch, the piper, was the

7

finest dance in the world, and I always held to a girl
that could airn her bread."

Well, Mike, he agreed with me on every p'int, only
he would not have his colleen to go in on the flure with
the mother, who was livin' with me at the same time.

I towld him punctually that I'd never shew the
ould mother the dure, and on that we nearly split, but
me sister, Jenny, who married Mike Dougherty's son's
wife's brother, came, and she says, says she, "let the
ould mother come live with me, where she'll always
have a hearty welcome, and an eye after the little gos-
soons when meself is out."

Well, it was fixed that way, and a fine weddin' we
had, sorra less, roast beef and swate cake, and lashins of
whiskey, and the height of good luck; and the finest
family we've had since, and a complater couple there

is n't on the townland. But after and all, Biddy has
one failin'; she 's a shockin' dhramer, the shockin'ist
dhramer ever I come across.   There 's not a mornin',
good luck to her, but she 'll have this: "Oh, John, I
dhramed a dhrame;" and I 'll say, "Whisht, now,
Biddy," but she 'll have it out in the spite of me.

Faix! I believe if it was kep' in on her she 'd choke.
Well, one mornin', anyhow, she begun:

"John, I dhrame'd a quare dhrame."

"Now," says I to meself, "John, you are in for it,
any way."

"Yes, John," said she, "I dhramed a dhrame, and
when I dhrame it 's sure to come in true," says she.

"Oh," says I, "sometimes it does, and more times
it does n't."

"Well," says she, "any way I dhramed a dhrame,
and in my dhrame I seen two black rats lookin' across
the wall.   The black rats is inimies, John, and the wall
is your purtection.   Then all of a suddint I seen their
fiery eyes lookin' at you.   That showed they were fierce
agin you.

"Then I saw that one had on Jack Dooner's new
frieze coat, and the other Mike Farrel's ould caubeen;
that showed me who they were.   Then I saw they had
two long grinnin' teeth a-piece, and great claws, which
towld me they had a power to injure you.   So then I
jined to study the wall that was your purtection, John,
and I seen that it was hung all over with Father Pether's
robes and vistmints; so now, John, take heed to what I
say, and whatsomever there is betuxt John Dooner, Mike

Farrell and yourself, tell it all fair and straight to Father Pether."

"Ah, don't be botherin' us," says I; and I knowin' well what she meant.

"Tell it all to Father Pether," says she.

"Hould your tongue," says I; and with that I tuk up my hat, and out I walked.

"You'll have no luck till ye do," she shouted after me.

Well, I went on to land the praties, but what she said stuck in me mind the whole mortial day; not that meself ever gave in to her dhrames, but it happened that the week before, Mike Farrell, Dooner and meself, whose farms all mearined with that villain Duff's big farm, had a differ with Duff about mendin' the gaps, and we left it on Father Pether to arbithrate, and he give it agin us.

So we swore we'd pull the wizends out of every Duff on the townland, and tar and feather Father Pether himself; and we were due to do it the same next night, it bein' Thursday, the market day of Ballycroughoo, and a holiday market, too, and Duff was to drive Father Pether on his own side car. Well, not a time I'd put in the loy to turn a sod that day, but I kep' twistin' it in my mind what I'd do, for I knew well that it was very disrespictful and a great liberty intirely for us to take with his Riverence, and still I felt loth to turn on me friends, and I knew they were both madder agin him nor I was meself, and that I would never turn them from their just revenge.

So, when I come in to my dinner, the wife says to me, says she:

"John, the praties are n't biled yet, nor won't this half hour; I had to bile an extra pot for the pigs, the crathurs, good luck to them, an' growin', an' thrivin', and 'atin' out of the face. They 're iligant feeders as iver I seen. Here 's yer Sunday hat, John," says she.

"What do I want with my Sunday hat," says I, but I tuk hoult of it, all the same, and out I stepped ag'in, and I says, "Biddy," says I, "if I do this, we must quit the counthry at onst."

"John," says she, and she took hoult of me two hands, "you 're an honest man, and are n't we under notice for non-payment of rent, and have n't I beyant sixty pounds in the ould stocking, and the childher are hardy, God bless 'em, and my father 'ud take the thrifle of stock off our hands; and supposin' we had to make a moonlight flittin' itself, what better could we do nor go to Ameriky, where I have siven first cousins an me great-grandmother Clark's side of the house, and more nor that of near friends. So, John, dear, don't let the boys tempt you to do anything agin your conscience;" and with that she pushed me through the dure, and off I went and tould Father Pether the whole business, and got full absolution, good luck to his Riverence.

"And now, John, you misfortunate crathur, what do you mane to be afther doin'?" says he, "for I know them fellows well, and afther this day's work yees can't stay here." So then I up and tould what Biddy said, and he wrote and tuk the passages for the whole of us, and we started two days after, by the assisted immigration, and that 's how Biddy's dhrame dhrove us all out of the counthry.

But we done right well ever since, and had no cause to regret it, for we throve apace, and the seven daughters made the best of good matches, and the boys did raal well, too, for I gave them an iligant education.

Biddy and meself takes no sort of throuble about anything now, but just sits and smokes our pipes in peace and comfort.

As to the ould counthry, I hear from all parts how all the neighbors regretted us so much that they boycotted the farm, and no one has dared to luk at it since, only them as lives close by grazes their cattle on it in peace and comfort; only ould Duff, which is a comfort to me, he is obligated to keep up his fences and not let a tail in on it.

So much for the ould counthry, which I still love in my heart, for there 's no land like it for real pleasure and friendliness and good-fellowship and neighborly, too; for if it had n't been for the neighbors, I 'd never have left it.

George H. Jessop.

TRUE LOVE'S TRIUMPH.

"'Farewell forever!'"

TRUE LOVE'S TRIUMPH.

[While the obvious trend of so much of our recent fiction is in the direction of anatomical realism, and concerns itself with expounding different phases of passion, or defining the ethics supposed to govern impromptu osculation, it is refreshing to note that the stories of which the following is modestly proffered as a model, still retain their pristine innocence of that blush-suffusing leaven which assails the cheeks of young persons from literature less immaculate. These stories lurk among the "patent insides" of country weeklies, affecting a position in the northwest corner of the third page, between a four-stanza poem on the Battle of Waterloo, and "Hints to Farmers."]

OF ALL THE GUESTS at the great seaside hotel, none excited more admiration than did John Hemlock and his beautiful fiancée, Valerian McIntosh.

Miss McIntosh was a superb creature, tall and stately, with a wealth of golden hair. Her eyes at times gave forth a cold, hard look, and her *hauteur* was chilling when she came in contact with those she deemed beneath her. Her nature was selfish; at least, so thought little Mary Bloggs, as she watched the pair. As John Hemlock, with his manly form, and refined, handsome face, hovered fondly over the chair of Miss McIntosh, it was evident he was enthralled by her beauty; and Mary suffered a good deal of anguish, for she had learned to love this man with all the wild, untrammeled fervor of her nature. It was the first love of her pure, young life; and when she saw how completely her idol was in the power of this heartless creature, how useless would be any attempt to reason with him, and point out his folly, it made her positively ill. She was a demure, shy little creature, with dark, wavy hair, and great questioning, brown eyes that prevented one from noting the other beauties of her face. Perhaps it was just as well.

John Hemlock had spoken to her casually a few times, with reference to the prevailing temperature; and then, how madly her poor little heart had beaten, until her soul seemed ready to burst from its prison, defy the cold formality that surrounded them, and mingle with his soul forever!

A pretty scene this would have made, right in front of the hotel; but that is how she felt, any how.

    *   *   *   *   *

"Of course, if matters are as you state, if your uncle has left you nothing but his old secretary, you are a poor man; and, for reasons which I will charitably refrain from enumerating, there is a permanency attaching to this condition, which impels me to seek a release from the troth I plighted when your financial perspective presented a more roseate hue."

The intelligent reader will identify the speaker, without hesitation.

"Ha, ha, perfidious one!" remarked John Hemlock, with hoarse conventionality, "you will never know how you have wrung my heart, and twisted and blackened some of the very finest chords in my nature. Henceforth, I shall be a cynical man of the world, and say awfully sarcastic remarks about your sex, like the dissipated noblemen in Ouida's novels. Farewell forever! I shall leave for a foreign shore, probably some time this evening."

He turned on his heel, a maneuver noticeably characteristic of the termination of heated interviews, and walked sadly away by himself (his invariable custom when he wished to be alone), cogitating, possibly, as to how closely his available assets would permit him to approximate that statement about the foreign shore. The cool evening breeze fanned his burning brow, and a number of stars glimmered some distance above him. From the open windows near by came bursts of laughter and intermittent fragments of song. He thought, with a bitter smile, that this gay life was no longer for him, and regretted that She was not there, to see how bitterly he could smile when he put his mind to it.

Suddenly the sounds of mirth subside, and a bird-like voice, clear as a bell, full of a rare, sympathetic tenderness, takes up the melody of an old Scotch song; and, as he listens, his being thrills with new life.

Mary Bloggs arose from the piano with all her inherent grace, leaving the piano where it was, however, and stepped out upon the dimly-lighted piazza. She started, as she saw John Hemlock's pale face.

"You appear ill," she said, not unkindly.

"It is nothing," he replied, brushing his hand across his forehead, as he had seen worried people do; "I have been listening to the voice of the girl I love. Oh, could you but know how that exquisite song has moved me!"

Poor little retiring Mary trembled strangely, and wondered what he would say next.

"Believe me," he said, "if I have, in the past, seemed to care for another. I was the victim of a delusion; the spell is broken, and I now see that I love but you."

"I, also, have loved you a great deal from the first, sir," said Mary, in quiet, well-bred tones; "and I have heard to-night of your deceased relative's testamentary remissness; but my love is far too noble, too unselfish to be hurt much by a thing like that."

And John Hemlock, in his new-found happiness, wondered how, for a moment, he could have fancied another.

"I am very poor," said Mary; "I used to canvass for an encyclopedia, but finding the pedestrianism and the emoluments it involved sadly disproportionate, I took up Art, and now support four infirm maiden aunts, also myself, by painting things for Brooklyn art dealers; but I am sure, dear, that, strengthened and guided by your love, I can help you to fight Life's battle;" and her voice was full of a strange sweetness, that touched John Hemlock.

"All right," he said, cheerfully; "and I will write magazine articles and critiques, though I will probably not receive more than six or eight thousand dollars' a year for the first few years; but after that, when I have had a little practice ——" and his face was flushed with a dawning knowledge of the latent possibilities he encompassed. "While it is true," and there came a far-away look into his eyes, "I had anticipated a somewhat different disposition of my uncle's fortune, I shall, nevertheless, accept my small inheritance in a becoming manner, and to-morrow I will run up to town and dispose of the old secretary. It will bring at least twelve dollars; but with you, darling," and his rich, manly tones bespoke infinite tenderness, "I would even be willing to face life empty-handed."

*   *   *   *   *

Two days later, John Hemlock returned.

"Are you sure you love me?" he asked her, anxiously. "Are you still willing to become a poor man's bride?"

"Ah yes indeed I am quite willing I assure you how can you ever doubt me?" said Mary Bloggs, with tremulous disregard for punctuation.

"Then, noble girl, behold your reward!" and John Hemlock waved before her astonished eyes a large roll of currency. "Here are nine million dollars, which I found hidden in a secret compartment of the old secretary; with this, and the income from my pen, I shall be enabled to support you in comparative affluence."

"Oh, is n't that nice!" said Mary, well nigh overcome; and she hid her head on his shoulder.

And no happier pair could be found in all the land, than John Hemlock and Mary Bloggs.

H. L. Wilson.

AUNT MARY'S OBITUARY.

"'Any new deaths, Jack?' enquired the editor."

AUNT MARY'S OBITUARY.

UST TEN O'CLOCK in the office of the *Beanville Clarion*, and by two the forms must be ready for the press. Seated in his easy-chair by the office stove, the editorial "We" lit a pipe and abandoned himself to a few moments of well-earned relaxation.

Secure in the consciousness that all the "locals" had been gathered in, that the first Spring batch of county snake stories had been read and corrected, and that Jack, the apprentice, was now on his way to the undertaker's shop to get a list of the deaths, the editor felt that he could well indulge in a fifteen minute smoke and meditation. There was nothing more to do except to write the death notices and to prepare whatever obituary paragraphs might be necessary.

"Any new deaths, Jack?" enquired the editor, as the apprentice entered the office.

8

"Yes," replied the boy, laying a bit of paper on the desk; "old Miss Larrabee died yesterday."

John Whittlesea, editor of the *Beanville Clarion*, leaped from his chair and then fell back into it, gasping for breath, while his face turned white and then red, and his hand shook as he tried to read the slip of dirty paper that lay on the desk before him.

There it was, plain enough, just as the boy had copied it from the silver plate in the undertaker's shop:

Mary Larrabee.
Born, 1851 — Died, 1890.

"Jack," said the editor, in an eager, excited voice; "are you sure you got this straight?"

"In course, I am," replied the boy; "I copied it off the coffin plate, same as I did the others, same as I always do."

"What sort of a coffin was it?"

"I did n't see no coffin. They was just a-finishing the plate."

"Likely enough it 's a pine one," rejoined the editorial Whittlesea. "She probably bargained for it with old Screws two weeks before she died. 'Born, 1851!' Surely, that must be a mistake. I 'll bet it 's 1831."

"No, 't ain't," declared Jack, sturdily. "I knowed she was older 'n that, so I looked at it twicet."

"Well, you go downstairs and tell Bill Clarke to keep the front page open for an obituary. He can put that clothing ad. in the other form."

Jack clattered off to the composing room, and

Whittlesea tilted back his chair, put his feet on the desk and began to think very industriously. Old Mary Larrabee had lived for more years than any one could remember in the rickety, rambling old homestead at the foot of Bald Cliff. The house had been built by her grandfather a dozen years before the Revolution. Her father had been born and had died in the south chamber over the family "settin'-room," and Mary, the last of her line, had never been for more than a week at a time out of the house in which she had drawn her first breath, and in which, since her father's death, she had dwelt alone with no companionship but that of her parrot and the neighbor who came in every day to help with the housework.

Old Mary Larrabee had but one blood relation in the world — her niece, Matilda — whom she had never forgiven for marrying against her wishes. That niece had married John Whittlesea, at that time a journeyman printer, and now editor and proprietor of the *Beanville Clarion.*

No; she had never forgiven poor Matilda, unless she had done so during the last week of her life, and that was a point that John Whittlesea was very curious about just at this moment, for the Larrabees had always been a thrifty and saving people, and there was no doubt that "Aunt Mary" was the possessor of a snug sum laid away in bank stocks and government bonds, to say nothing of the broad fertile acres that stretched from end to end of "Larrabee's Hollow."

"Where would all this property go if not to Matilda?" said John to himself, as he puffed gleefully away at his pipe. Then he turned white about the gills as he recalled Aunt Mary's fondness for a certain Home for Friendless Seventh Day Baptists in Hartford, to which she had once contributed six quilts of her own making, —a burst of generosity that set the whole neighborhood talking, and started the rumor that she had made her will in favor of that admirable charity. She certainly had been closeted with Squire Doolittle a whole afternoon a few days after the big bundle of quilts was expressed to the Hartford institution; but what had taken place during that interview, whether she had made a new will or altered an old one, was never revealed to the curious ones of Beanville. No one dared to ask the Squire, and as for Mary Larrabee, she was as tight as the traditional drum in regard to whatever concerned herself, though decidedly free with her tongue whenever any of the neighbors were being weighed in the balance.

"She *could* n't have had the heart to cut Matilda off entirely," meditated John. "I 'll bet she 's left that parrot of hers an income for the rest of its life. It 's the only thing that breathes she ever cared for. 'Born, 1851!' Why, Mary Larrabee was sixty-three last January—though she never would own to forty. I never *did* see any one as sensitive as she was about her age. I believe the real reason she was down on me was that paragraph I put in fifteen years ago about her birthday party. Well, it was a sort of mean dig, I 'll admit."

He smiled as he recalled her foolish endeavors to

pass for twenty-five years younger than she was, in the community in which she had been born and brought up.

John Whittlesea might have gone on with his meditations until two o'clock if he had not been awakened by a sharp demand for copy, shouted by the foreman through the speaking tube; and a moment later Jack appeared at the head of the stairs and said that the lady compositors wanted to know if there was to be any more matter to set that day.

"Yes," exclaimed the editor, suddenly bringing down his chair on four legs, and taking up his pen; "wait a minute and you can take down the first page of this obituary."

He was in a hopeful mood as he began the conventional paragraph about the "sad and unexpected removal from our midst of Miss Mary Larrabee, a member of one of the oldest families in the county, and a woman whose liberal and unostentatious charities —"

He smiled when he came to this, laid down his pen, reflected for a moment, and then tore the page up and started afresh. He had written and sent downstairs three or four pages of manuscript — enough to keep the lady compositors quiet for a few minutes — when the absurdity of what he was writing suddenly struck him. There was not a man, woman or child in the whole county who did not know exactly how he stood in regard to Aunt Mary Larrabee, and how ridiculous it must seem to them to read his edifying remarks about the "grief-stricken relatives bowing in resignation to the Divine Will."

"If I tried to write a comic obituary it could n't be funnier than that."

He took up his pen again, and a malicious grin spread over his features as he wrote the concluding pages of the notice.

"There," he said to the boy, "have that set up right away, and then the forms can go to press. Don't forget to leave a couple of papers at my house. I 've got to go out to Bricktop Corners and won't be back till late in the afternoon."

It was nearly five o'clock when John Whittlesea reached home and found his wife waiting for him on the doorstep.

"O John!" she cried; "what *do* you think has happened? Aunt Mary —"

"I know, dear," he responded; "I heard about it downstreet, and you 'll find it all in the paper this after-noon. When is the funeral to be?"

"They 're going to bury her to-morrow, and we must go. Aunt Mary was here herself to tell us about it, only half an hour ago — why, what 's the matter, John? Are you sick?"

The editor of the *Clarion* was leaning against the house, with a face as white as chalk.

"Aunt Mary was here half an hour ago to invite us to attend her own funeral?" he gasped.

"No; the funeral of her parrot, which died yester-day. And she says she 's no one but us to love, now that the bird has gone, and she 's going to bury her in a beautiful rose-wood coffin, with her name on a silver

plate; and she asked how you were getting along, and I
left her in the parlor looking over to-day's paper the boy
brought up for you. She seemed real interested; but
when I came back she 'd gone away. Why, what 's the
matter, John?"

"Matter enough," replied the editor; "let me see
that paper. Yes; I thought so. Read that obituary, and
tell me what you think of the last paragraph."

The paragraph read as follows:

"Our grief and agitation as we pen these hurried
lines can only be appreciated by those who have been
similarly afflicted. To lose a wife's aunt, and be uncer-
tain whether the hoardings of sixty years will enrich the

editorial coffers or swell the fund for the preservation of friendless Seventh Day Baptists is a grief of bitterness which is like that of death itself; and not until this matter has been decided will the editorial head lie easy on its pillow."

J. L. Ford.

INTERNECINE COMPARISON.

"A most interesting game of poker."

INTERNECINE COMPARISON.

E WERE IN CAMP at Newport News, and my tent had been unluckily pitched on as the *rendez-vous* for about all the harum-scarum lights of the regiment. Matters bellicose had been so quiet for a month that the men were getting careless and uneasy. The officers had planned more fake campaigns, and partaken of more "Sutler's Squeeze" than was conducive to the best of discipline; and, taken all around, there was a spirit of happy-go-luckiness in the air, ill fitting the seriousness of the complications that had brought us into soldiering.

Tom Kelso's mother had sent him a box of circular-pressed Damascus figs some weeks before the transport left New York, and as the package had been billed by mistake to Newport, Kentucky, and from there to Newport, Rhode Island, prior to its getting on the right track, and had lain in the store-house at the News, marked beyond recognition, for two months after our arrival, the fruit had assumed a consistency-and polish suggestive, I am sorry to say, of a fair quality of poker-chips.

The resemblance was quickly noted as soon as the box was opened; and after Tom had worn the enamel from a tooth and English expletives out in an effort to be filial, he turned the case over to the mess; and one evening found the condiments stacked at a quarter a-piece on the four respective corners of the Adjutant's table.

As I was the Adjutant, courtesy would not permit me to object, and with Tom as first dealer, the Doctor as "age," and the old Colonel as the "blind," a most interesting game of poker was soon under way.

Like most similar games, it had its ups and downs, and at the end of three hours I had to buy a double stack, and start in anew.

The Colonel, who was banking, had eaten several of the softer of his chips by this time; but he was good for any reasonable amount, and as he could, by no possibility, eat them fast, we said nothing, and the game went on.

This is not a poker story, so that those who have followed it along in the expectation of reading of some

phenomenal winning on a "rag-end-flush," or
of a jack-pot that stacked up so high that
it lifted the tent ridge-pole, will, like
many side-column readers of the press,
be patent-medicined.

I only wanted to give a phase
of human nature, which introduced itself just after my second
investment, when the Colonel was
called out by an orderly to look at
a suspicious package for the sutler,
marked "hymnals."

The Colonel was a gentleman,
and a brave and gallant soldier;
but by some accident, either hereditary
or otherwise, he was fitted with a head
shaped more than anything else like an immense pear set on his neck, so that his nose
answered for the stem.

As hands were laid down, and he disappeared
through the tent-flap, Kelso observed:

"I 've traveled to a considerable extent, and as a
diligent observer have noted a great many people, but
that man has got the queerest-shaped head of any one
I ever came across. Wonder what kind of spasm struck
Nature when she flag-topped him like that."

Just then the Colonel appeared again, and the
entrance of his face through the canvas aperture *did*
suggest a sun-fish ploughing through a wave. The
game was continued, until a little later the Doctor was

called out to attend a man who had snapped the gun-lock on his finger in an effort to light his pipe from a percussion cap. Hands went down again, and the Colonel observed:

"There goes a good surgeon and a good man, but he's got the blamedest looking nose I ever saw. Looks as if it had been caught in a muskrat trap. Of course, I would n't ask him for the world what the matter is with it, but I 'd give a month's pay to know.

"Pass that throat-vase, will you, Tom?" and the bric-à-brac went around.

The Doctor came in presently, and once more the flip-flap of paste-board went on.

At last Kelso stretched himself with a yawn, after a loss, when he had confidently expected to win, and said:

"Boys, let 's make this a progressive game. I 'm all tired out. We 'll let the bank just stand as it is, with debts and credits recorded, and resume again to-morrow night where we left off."

This was agreed to, in spite of the unkind suspicion that Tom failed to have the necessary amount to cash up with, and he went out into the darkness.

"Did you ever notice anything peculiar about Tom?" asked the Doctor.

"Yes; I have," replied the Colonel, "and I never could determine just what it was. He has got an open, pleasant face, but there is something lacking in it; and I 've watched him many a time, trying to think out what that something is."

"Why, man alive," resumed the Doctor, "he ain't got an eyebrow to his name. Bald-faced above the bridge of his nose as a soap-bubble. Funny you never tumbled to it, Colonel."

With this, the two old war-horses gathered themselves together and sought their own quarters.

As the lantern was put out, and I crawled into my bunk, I wondered whether I, myself, had any uncouth characteristic which might cause comment in a temporary absence; and just as I was losing myself in a dream of home, I heard my sentinel murmur in an undertone to his comrade on the next beat:

"Don't shuffle so on the turn, podner! Ole Torch-whisker Jim 's tryin' t' sleep off his beauty!"

James S. Goodwin.

A DRAWN BATTLE.

"Soon Dash began to weaken."

A DRAWN BATTLE.

THOUGHT I did a very clever thing when I invited Miss Hawkins, Mr. Dash and a few other friends to take a sail in my yacht. I say "my" yacht, because I was entitled to her for that day, because of my owning a third of her; and I do not give the names of the other friends, because they were only meant to fill in the background. Still, I will mention one gentleman of the supernumeraries. Mr. Vincent was one of the party, and he was a very welcome addition to the number. Everybody liked Vincent. He was the sort of man who gave tone to any set of people. It is difficult to say exactly why, for really he had no "points." He was quiet, rather dignified, and of a good figure — the sort of figure which enables one to wear ready-made clothes without explaining why one prefers them. I have nothing to say against Vincent, even now.

But Dash was different. He was really clever and knowing. But he had his limitations. Yachting was

one of them. He did n't know a sharpie from a lugger,
and that 's the reason I gave the yachting party.

You see, Dash had confided to me that he thought
Miss Hawkins was a "stunner." That is the way he
put it. He did n't confide in me because I was his
particular confidant and crony, but only because I happened to be with him when his intellect, so to speak,
came to the conclusion that she was a "stunner."

I did not disagree with him. In fact, I thought
then, as I think now, that Miss Hawkins threw into a
cooling shade any young woman of her time. For that
reason, I got up the yachting party.

Miss Hawkins accepted with pleasure; and when I
told Dash that she was coming, he said he would
accept with pleasure, too. Now, that was not
true. Dash hated the salt water, and only went
because he knew he would be green with jealousy if he should stay at home.

It was a charming day for a sail — the
water was gently rippling against the side of
the boat when we started, but there were tiny
white caps showing just beyond the headlands which
flanked the harbor.

Miss Hawkins sat upon a canvas chair on deck, and
Dash and I were beside her, engaged in a sprightly
small-talk competition. Poor victim! By easy stages
I led him on until he was fairly launched in wild career.

"Yes, Miss Hawkins," said he; "there is, as you
say, a certain wild sense of exhilaration in sailing upon
the free blue sea."

"I said," she answered with a smile, "that I had always heard so. But I have had but little experience in sailing. I feel very grateful to Mr. Seaborn for an opportunity of enjoying this delicious breeze and bright sunshine."

I sighed a gentle acknowledgment and bowed.

"But, after all," Dash broke in, hastily; "one finds the same pleasure in driving."

"Oh, *do* you think so?" answered Miss Hawkins.

"Well, perhaps—there may be certain features of sailing which one might prefer," he replied, weakly enough.

Just then we passed the lee of one of the headlands, and the yacht began to jump. Everything worked to a charm. The boat would lift her forefoot gracefully against the oncoming wave, the wave would slide under the keel, and the boat would come down with a thump. And at every thump Dash would wilt. I said very little, and kept well in the background, so that he was compelled to devote himself to Miss Hawkins. Vincent was devoting his efforts to entertaining Miss Hawkins's aunt, a most agreeable chaperon. That was always the way with Vincent—he could be depended upon.

Soon Dash began to weaken; he grew pale, and his conversation lost all vivacity. Full of solicitude I hovered about him. I suggested that he would feel better if he should go forward and lie down.

Of course, he would n't, and his conversation soon became perfectly inane. Being at my best on a yacht, he was soon nowhere, and I had the field all to myself.

I named the interesting points along shore; explained that marvelous invention, the mariner's compass; showed how the boat ran against the wind, or came about; taught Miss Hawkins to steer; gave peremptory orders to the skipper and crew; superintended the dainty luncheon on deck, and sympathized properly with poor Dash, who had long since gone below.

That settled Dash. When we rounded to at the moorings, I think Dash may be said to have been out of it. He went at once to his rooms, a pale, ghastly and utterly uninteresting land-lubber, while Vincent and I escorted home the Miss Hawkins contingent.

After the ladies had gone in, Vincent turned to me and said significantly:

"Seaborn, did you know that Dash was so poor a sailor?"

"Well," I said, lightly; "he said he would be delighted to come — but I think he made a mistake."

"Yes," he answered, in his solemn way; "Miss Hawkins asked me to tell 'poor Mr. Dash' how sorry she was for him."

But Dash did n't know when he was whipped. So he got up a coaching party. That was ingenious, too; for he did n't say anything about it beforehand, and I supposed it was only an ordinary picnic — a luncheon in the woods. Then he arranged things so as to have Miss Hawkins and myself seated with him on the front seat, while, as was inevitable, Vincent and the aunt were behind us. I did n't suspect anything until we had gone a few miles into the country, and then he asked me to take the reins for a few moments, while he went to help the footman fasten one of the hampers. No sooner had he reached the back of the tally-ho, than he called out:

"All right, Seaborn, go ahead. There is none too much time. I can fix this while we drive along!"

Then was my time to rise, and say frankly and simply:

"But, Mr. Dash, I never drove anything but an old family hack. I shall have to decline."

Perhaps you would have done so. I did n't. I made a ghastly click, and that awful menagerie in leather sprang into life.

I think I shook like an aspen. My head whirled, and the road looked like a black mist. Miss Hawkins said something quickly, and I turned to hear what it was, and dropped a rein.

Vincent must have climbed down into Dash's vacant seat and stopped the maddened steeds, I am sure; for the next thing I knew, they were standing all in a bunch, head to head.

Then I volunteered to fasten the hamper; and long after that hamper was fastened like a safe-deposit security box, I sat there on that back seat with the footmen.

Thus did *I* take a back seat.

And, to be perfectly fair, I think I was out of it from that moment.

＊　　　＊　　　＊　　　＊　　　＊

I don't blame Miss Hawkins, for, may be, neither Dash nor I stood a ghost of a show. Hereafter, if I meet another "stunner," I shall devote myself to a waiting-race with the chaperon, and leave it to others to set the pace and make the running.

I don't mind a sail," I answered, "on a quiet day."

We dined at the Vincents not long ago, and, really, they seemed so happy that I think Dash and I both resolved to bury the hatchet. At all events, as we were coming away, Dash said:

"After all, there is nothing pleasanter than a quiet dinner with a pleasant host and hostess. I think these out-door sports and entertainments are an awful bore, you know!"

"Well, I don't mind a sail," I answered, "on a quiet day."

"Yes, in a calm," said he, laughing; "but a good, brisk drive is the real thing."

"With another fellow to hold the ribbons," I suggested.

We spent the evening playing double dummy at the club.

Tudor Jenks.

THE MAGIC CITY.

"*A messenger came to summon Petrudio
to peel potatos for dinner.*"

THE MAGIC CITY.

A Romance of the Twentieth Century.

Chaps. I to VIII.

ORCIVAL. DE TWIRLIGER goes to Honduras as special agent for the New York Suspender Co. (Limited.) Firm speculates in new style of buckles and goes up. Orcival starts to hoof it to New York. Various adventures. Separated from companion in wilds of Mexico. Lost on the desert. Great heavens! it is sad to die thus. What does he see? — a city! Goes for it. Meets venerable man with long beard.

Chap. IX.

(NOTE. — *Story now begins. Prior portion put in to make the book sell for $1.50.*)

"I do not wonder at your surprise," said Petrudio, "although our city has been established twenty years. It was founded by Edward Bellamy, Sergius Stepniak, Joaquin Miller and Jules Verne. It is a paradise upon earth, where everything is in common, and where everybody works and is happy. We have no laws, because there is no crime."

"Does no one ever break loose just for the fun of the thing?" inquired De Twirliger.

"Never," replied Petrudio, with a patronizing smile.

"Suppose they did?" persisted De Twirliger.

"The supposition is inadmissible," returned the patriarch, sternly; "all people who live in the Magic City have divested themselves of love, hate, envy, ambition or desires of any kind."

"Something like a wooden image," suggested De Twirliger, winking at a young girl who floated past in an aluminium balloon.

"How are the soft snaps in the working line distributed?"

"All take their turns; there is no jealousy. In our community, work is a pleasure."

At this moment a messenger came to summon Petrudio to peel potatos for dinner.

Chaps. X to XXVI.

Aluminium balloons — glass railways — electric lights, tubes, chutes and conveyances — machines to make rain — free concerts and theatrical performances by angelic singers and supernaturally gifted actors — no doctors or lawyers — complicated harangues about isms, æons, ologies and flub-dub.

Chap. XXVII.

"Say!" exclaimed Orcival De Twirliger, with a capacious yawn; "this is turning sour. Honest Injun, Petrudino, would n't you like to be a man and own yourself for a month or two?"

"I have occasionally thought," said Petrudio, stopping up a near-by speaking tube with the tail of his toga, "that this model city racket is being carried too far. A lot of old seeds with chin whiskers and the virility of a turnip might meander through life in this community, but a man with blood in his veins has no business to turn himself into a machine. Now I am thirty-two — "

"I took you to be one hundred and sixteen," remarked De Twirliger; "your beard and gown — "

"That is the model city regulation; they all do it. It gives a patriarchal and gliding air to the people. To return : — thirty-two, with the prospect of gliding and floating around for a half century, without a cent in my pockets, putting up stove-pipes one day and painting pictures the next, living a life of solid, unadulterated virtue, and not even allowed to choose an affinity."

"I thought you all had affinities?"

"So we have.   There is an annual drawing at the City Hall for affinities, and the one I drew last year would curdle the milk of human kindness."

"The beautiful Etudia and I," said De Twirliger, calmly, "are about to elope if we can steal the grand patriarch's balloon. If you can hook on to an affinity of your own choosing, we may make room for you as ballast."

"There is a stout German girl who is detailed to dust the palace this month," said Petrudio, musingly.   "She squeezed my hand at the last mush - and - milk sociable, and made some earthly remark about giving the whole boiling for a glass of beer. If you'll give me twenty-four hours, I'll see if I can make a vacancy in the colony."

Chaps. XXVIII, XXIX and XXX.

Various monkeyings around to keep the reader in suspense.

Chaps. XXXI and XXXII.

The flight of De Twirliger and the beautiful Etudia, accompanied by Petrudio (with his whiskers cut off) and Loreeta.   Crossing the desert.   Water gives out — got

to give out — everybody forgives everybody else, and all
about to die in holy calm, when the balloon falls into
Lake Pontchartrain.

Chap. XXXIII.

"Well," said Orcival, as the quartet sat at table in
the dining-room of the St. Charles, "it is bad form to
notice one's eating, but from the way you destroyed that
steak, Etudia, I should judge that roses and dew are not
the only fare worth living for."

Etudia showed her pearly teeth, but was too happy
to make reply. Loreeta, meanwhile, had ordered her
third piece of pie.

Petrudio, who had been
silent up to this point, now
said, gravely :

"Orcival, let us
lift in some pale brandy
to settle this repast,
and then for a good
old smoke."

Half an hour later
they were playing billiards.

"After all," said Petru-
dio, after a run of ten, "life is
only enjoyable when you have
to hustle and know that you can keep what you can
grab. Without rivalry, there can be no material progress. A man of spirit had better peddle shoestrings

than link himself with cranks who surrender their brains to an idea that won't work."

"And how fortunate," said Orcival, "that I relieved the colony of several bags of dross. It was only in their way, while we can put it where it will do the most good."

Sidney.

MR. WILKENNING'S HOBBY.

"'Calling on all the people he ever heard of, to get points on farming.'"

MR. WILKENNING'S HOBBY.

"MARY; I'm going to quit business."

Miss Wilkenning, sewing away with nimble fingers and engrossed in her own thoughts, had not noticed that her brother had ceased reading; and this abrupt remark startled her. She looked up quickly and met his calm gaze.

"Quit business!" she exclaimed. "What do you mean?"

Mr. Wilkenning laid his paper on the table, put his hands in his trousers' pockets and crossed his legs, while his sister waited.

"I mean," he said, when he had adjusted himself satisfactorily, "that I'm going to turn over the whole thing to Wharton and retire; go out; quit."

"But, Alfred! you're only forty-six years old!"

"I've got money enough."

"But you're an active, energetic man. What will you do with yourself when you have no business to attend to?"

Mr. Wilkenning elevated his eyebrows. " I 'll enjoy myself," he said in a contemplative tone. " I 'll let
my inclinations lead me about from one thing to another
for a while, and perhaps — by and by — I 'll take a little
ride on my hobby."

Miss Wilkenning slowly gathered up the work in
her lap and placed it on the table, while her brother
lowered his eyes from the ceiling and looked at her with
a half furtive expression on his good-humored face.

" Alfred," said Miss Wilkenning solemnly, folding
her hands in her lap; " you are going to give up business on purpose to go into the country and buy a farm.
You have had that on your mind for two years — ever
since you gave Mr. Wharton a half interest in the business.

" You look back to the days of your boyhood, and
you imagine that you could again be as happy and free
as you were then. You don't consider that the conditions have changed; that you have changed. You will
relinquish all the comforts, all the luxuries you have
been accustomed to here, all the friends whose society is
a pleasure, an incentive to you; you will go away from
the city and *rust out* in some isolated country place,
among narrow, plodding people whom you can not
sympathize with or care for.

" It is folly.

" Why won't you put the idea out of your head
and be contented where you are certain to be happiest?"

Mr. Wilkenning arose and walked two or three times
across the room. Then he stopped in front of his sister.

"Mary," said he; "the love of the country was born in me. I have lost sight of that fact while I slaved at business; but now, when I am able to free myself, a longing for the old life comes back to me with a force you can't understand.

"I've trotted around on slabs of stone for as many years as I care to. I'd give ten dollars this minute if I just could take off my varnished boots and silk stockings and plant my bare feet on the damp, cold turf.

"I'd give five years of my life in this overcrowded, ill-smelling city of steaming sewer-pipes for one year of blessed stillness in a place where the sun shines on the earth and not on the tin roofs of office-buildings and tenement houses."

Mr. Wilkenning took another turn around the room and stopped, facing his sister again.

"Every chestnut-tree in the pasture lot" — he went on — "every apple-tree in the orchard — every old zig-zag fence on that farm is everlastingly fixed in my memory; and they seem to be waiting for me to come back."

He stopped abruptly and then added:

"But you don't want to go, Mary."

Miss Wilkenning took her work off the table and began to sew again.

"I am making some warm clothes for one of my children," she said; "you know I have forty-seven of them. What would they do if I should go away?"

"Ah, yes! your mission. *You* have a hobby, too. I had forgotten that."

Miss Wilkenning looked earnestly into her brother's face.

"Alfred," she said; "you are tired of your home life. You are tired of seeing nothing but this old maid's face morning and evening, year after year. You don't know it, but that is the trouble. If you were married and had a family around you, you would be happy and —"

"Stop!"

Miss Wilkenning would have stopped about here, anyhow; for her voice and lips were tremulous. Her brother came around to the back of her chair.

"Let's see that old maid's face," he said; and he took it between his hands.

"*You* are the one that ought to have a husband and a house full of children to love and care for," he said; "you are wasting your life on a cranky old bachelor brother. It's a shame — a downright shame! But there!" — he kissed her — "I couldn't get along without you; no; I could not, possibly. I have not thought of such a thing as a wife, Mary, in twenty-five years. I don't want a wife. I wouldn't have one around. Now, let's stop our nonsense about getting married, and talk of something that is among the possibilities.

"And here is one theme — your unreasoning prejudice against the country. I'm going to remove that or else I'm going to give up to it. I have a scheme which will result in one of those two things. Want to hear it?"

Miss Wilkenning bowed her head.

"Well, I'm going up to Ryefields, Massachusetts,

among the farmers — those plodding farmers who never leave their homes for three days at a time; and I'm going to hunt up the brightest, most progressive one of them all; and I'm going to ask him to come here and stay two weeks — do you follow me? — to stay two weeks as our guest.

"If he turns out to be a wide-awake, agreeable, well-bred man, one whose intellectual attainments are up to your standard, then you've got to acknowledge that that kind of people *can* grow in the country, and that *I* might live in the country without getting rusty. If I can't find such a man, then we'll stay in New York.

"How 's that?

"If I 've taken your breath away, I 'll wait till you get it back. Take your time."

Mr. Wilkenning sat down and pretended to read the paper. When he sought his sister's face again, she was gazing at him with an amused smile.

"Well?" said he.

"I 'll accept that test," she said; "but I wonder if you have any particular person in mind. Do you think of any one of your country acquaintances who would be likely to convert me?"

"I 've thought of several young fellows whom I knew years ago, Mary. There 's that third or fourth cousin of ours, Tom Beverly, for one. He 's a bright sort of fellow, eh?"

"He was — fifteen years ago."

"I wonder how he 'd do for a test case!"

"You can call on him and see."

"He's living there with his sister, Grace, is n't he?"

"Yes; I wonder why neither of them married?"

"Had too much sense. Well, they ought to be a typical country pair by this time; but I'll wager that Tom Beverly is as bright as a new dollar. I'll take those two for my subjects. I'll ask 'em both to come down to see us. That's exactly what I'll do; and I'll go up there to-morrow morning."

"You're not wasting any time, Alfred. How long shall you stay?"

"Can't tell. These plodding people are hard to move, you know; they may need a deal of coaxing. You must n't be alarmed if I'm gone two or three days."

"All right," said Miss Wilkenning.

The conversation ceased, and Mr. Wilkenning began once more to pace the floor. His face was radiant, and his tread was quick and elastic. The contemplation of a visit to Ryefields filled him with joy.

*　　*　　*　　*　　*

And Mr. Wilkenning went to Ryefields on the following day. He announced his arrival there in a letter to his sister, from which the following is an extract:

*　*　* *But is n't it a very singular coincidence that Tom Beverly should have left here for New York at the very time I was starting for Ryefields. Grace says he has been talking of visiting New York for a year or two; and finally, he made a sudden resolve to go, and posted himself off. He intended to go straight to our house; and of course you kept him there. How*

*do you like him? I shall not tell you what sort of a
woman Grace is, though; you must wait until you
see her.* * * * *They have a magnificent farm, and
I'm not going to leave it for a day or two, now that
I've got up here. Tell Tom that, and keep him until
I come home. Give him this letter of introduction to
Wharton, and tell him to make himself at home at the
office as well as at the house. When I get back, I'll
take him around to see the sights. Grace says he has
had a great longing to visit the city — thinks he'd like
to live there; and I believe it worries her a little. Don't
let him get into mischief.*

The answer to this letter was in part as follows:

* * * *But don't stay too long. If you won't
tell me about Grace, I think I'll not take the trouble
to describe Tom for you.* * * * * *I should say
he did like the city. He's a regular boy. You'll
have very little to show him, unless you hurry to come
home; for he is "taking in the town" pretty thoroughly.* * * * * *He says you will find Dolly a
fine animal to drive, if you want fire; but you must
keep a close eye on her. Gray Ned, he says, is a good
road horse, too, but more moderate. I think you'd
better use the gray horse, and let the other one alone.
Shall you be home soon?*

It was two or three days after this was written,
when Thomas Beverly, in the city, got a letter from his
sister.

He says, every day, he's going home to-morrow,
she wrote; *but he does n't go. He is driving over the
country, calling on all the people he ever heard of, to
get points on farming, he says. I do believe he was
cut out for a farmer. Yesterday, Mr. Hendricks came
down from Clearbrook to look at those yearlings, and
Mr. Wilkenning took him in hand and sold him seven
of them and the sorrel colt. I told him how much you
expected to get, and he did better by about seventy dollars. Did you forget your appointment with Mr. Hendricks? How much longer are you going to stay in
New York?*

Nearly a week more elapsed, and then Mr. Wilkenning, at Ryefields, received a short letter from his sister,
closing with these words: *Alfred, you* MUST *come home.*

And Mr. Wilkenning did come home. He reached
New York very early in the morning, arriving at the

house before his sister had come downstairs. His guest, however, was in the library, with morning paper spread out before him.

"Say, you 're a great fellow!" exclaimed Mr. Beverly, when the two had greeted each other with genuine warmth; "why did n't you stay up there? I wanted to have a quail-hunt with you."

"The deuce you did!" said Mr. Wilkenning. "Why did n't you say so? I 'd have staid. But I 've come home to entertain you — *partly* — and partly because Mary wrote me that I *must* come."

"She did n't, though?" said Mr. Beverly, with a peculiar expression of countenance.

"She did, though," said Mr. Wilkenning. "What do you find of interest in the paper this morning, Tom?"

Mr. Beverly had suddenly buried his face in the newspaper.

"I was just looking up a little advertisement of mine," he said; "I — I — to tell the truth, Alf, I 'm desperately in love with New York, and I 've offered a — a desirable country place in exchange for —" (he was searching for the advertisement) "for a city house. Here 't is. Want to read it?"

"Do you deal with brokers or owners?" inquired Mr. Wilkenning.

"Owners; positively."

"Then I 'll talk with you. I want that farm of yours."

"The deuce you do!"

"Will you swap places?"

"Yes," said Mr. Beverly, throwing his paper aside; "I will."

"Even?"

"Yes; even."

"It 's a go!"

They grasped hands.

"My sister can't bear to think of leaving New York, though," said Mr. Wilkenning, with a troubled look.

"She won't have to," said Mr. Beverly, tightening

his grip; "we 've settled that. It 's tough on you, old fellow, and she — she 's cried over it a lot, Alf, I know she has, and I believe she 's afraid to meet you; but don't reproach her, old man. You 'll get used to it. Brothers and sisters can't always —"

He hesitated.

"Go on," said Mr. Wilkenning, whose expression was anything but reproachful: "what were you saying about brothers and sisters?"

"I was thinking about *my* sister," said Mr. Beverly; "it would break her heart to leave Ryefields."

"Tom," cried Mr. Wilkenning, "she won't have to!"

"What!"

"We've settled that."

"Is it a swap?"

"It is."

"Even?"

"Even!"

And Miss Wilkenning, coming softly down the stairs at this moment, found these two big fellows clasped in each other's arms.

C. H. Augur.

THE CASHIER AND THE BURGLAR.

•

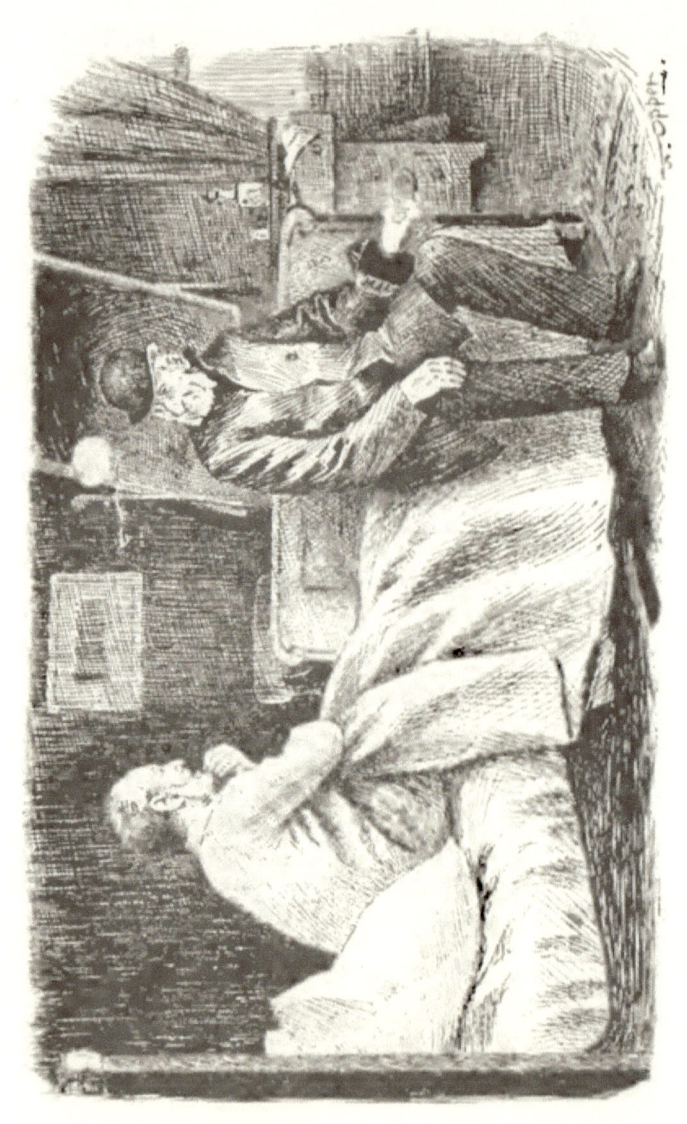

" 'Does burglary pay?' asked Horatius."

THE CASHIER AND THE BURGLAR.

MR. HORATIUS LYMAN, the esteemed cashier of the Merchants' Bank of Diggsville, was a light sleeper; and at the tread of cautious footsteps, he carefully opened his eyes to see on the wall a wavering spot of light, an illumination which he instantly reasoned could only proceed from a dark lantern.

Glancing as carefully sideways, he beheld, bending over his top drawer and bestowing on its contents a calm and impartial investigation, the lantern's burglarious owner.

By a slight, backward pressure of the head, Mr. Lyman assured himself that his watch, his rings, his revolver, and certain other valuables, were still under his pillow, where he had placed them; and, being himself of a calm temperament, he made no further movement, but quietly watching his felonious visitor, permitted himself the novel amusement of mapping out the methods which a scientific burglar might be expected to follow.

To his great satisfaction, he succeeded for fully ten minutes in anticipating every move the burglar made; but he was forced to confess to himself that it was, after

all, an easy task; as during that time the burglar was
wholly occupied with the bureau drawer, and with his,
Mr. Lyman's, trousers.

"Will he," inquired Mr. Lyman of himself; "will he next take up the es-
critoire, or the dime savings bank
on the mantel-piece? For my
own part, I should avoid
dimes. There is not enough
in them to compensate for
their rattle."

These last words Mr. Ly-
man so far forgot himself as
to murmur half aloud. The
burglar instantly turned the
dark lantern full in his face,
and he was caught with his eyes
open. Most unexpected was the re-
sult. The burglar gave a loud exclamation of surprise,
and at once shut off the light.

"Well, what's the matter?" asked Mr. Lyman,
calmly feeling for his revolver.

"Are you a looking glass?" the burglar inquired,
in subdued tones, flashing the light again into Mr.
Lyman's whiskers.

"Hardly," returned the cashier.

"Then," said the burglar, ruefully, "you are my
twin brother, Horatius Lyman, and I've simply got to
return the swag and stand a moral lecture. Hang it, I'm
perfectly sick of this business. It rushes a man to death,

and jogs his conscience till a toothache seems like a holiday. What possessed you to come and live here, Horatius?"

Mr. Lyman was pleased with his brother's frankness of speech.

"Albert," he said, "I never should have recognized you, for you were behind the light. Now, if you will turn it on yourself for a minute — thank you. Extraordinary resemblance, is n't it — even to the length of the whiskers! But Albert, I thought you were keeping a grocery store in New York. How do you happen to be here to-night?"

"Children," said Albert, gloomily. He had now seated himself on the edge of the bed.

"But, Albert," said Horatius, hastily, "you are not married?"

The grocer-burglar shook his head.

"Never a marry," he said; "if I had had a wife, she might have kept me straight. You see, I tried to attract custom by baiting for the shopping kid — the child sent on errands — and for children out shopping with their mothers. I left all the boxes of raisins, nuts, figs, crackers and so on, open, and kept a stock of playthings, which I threw in with purchases. Then I would say:

"'To you, Madam, eight cents a pound; but if I were selling to this little dear, I should say seven.'

"The idea worked like an eyelet-hole machine at first, and I developed it. It was a great success. Every day except Monday — wash-day, you know — the store was crowded. It was n't for six months, and money coming in all the time, that I began to realize what I'd done.

"My dear sir, the children ate up my profits twice as fast as I made them. The women got wind of my plan, and they brought their whole families in at lunch-time and staid, asking prices till the kids were gorged on crackers and cheese and almonds and ginger-bread.

"As for cutting prices to the babies, after the first two weeks I didn't make a sale to a single adult. Those who had no children borrowed them to come and shop. A wife might have foreseen this — but I, a bachelor, had ruined myself. What was I to do except to take to burglary, nights, and to try to keep my head above water that way? And it takes all the running round I do to keep even, I can tell you."

"My poor brother," said Horatius, "how unfortunate! And is this really true?"

"I don't sit up at nights to tell fairy stories," said Albert, gloomily. "I spent fifty dollars last week in crackers alone."

The cashier shook his head sorrowfully.

"Never," he said, "was a man waked up at midnight to be confronted with a more painful situation. I shall not lecture you, Albert. Your story is too sad. But was there no way except burglary?"

"None that I saw," Albert said.

"If I could help you," said Horatius. "I should grudge no labor. Nor does the problem seem to me desperate. Yet I can not help thinking," he mused, "that you should have started a drug store."

"I believe," said Albert, moodily, "that I will let the grocery go, and take to burglary out and out. In that way I should at least make up my sleep."

"Does burglary pay?" asked Horatius.

Albert started at the question.

"Why do you ask that?" he said, suspiciously. "You 're not short in your accounts, are you?"

"No," said Horatius, with a smile. "To tell the truth, I was thinking that you had not mastered your profession, or you would not be wasting your time over my bureau drawers when you ought to be clearing out the bank downstairs."

"Right enough," said the moody Albert. "I dare say I 'm an amateur. By the way, here are your keys, which I have not yet returned."

"Again," Horatius resumed, taking the keys, "you are equally short-sighted as a grocer. You give to the children, but you do not make the mothers pay."

"I can not contradict you there," the other replied. "Why, why did we drift apart? Why have I been all these years without your counsel?"

"Really, it seems to me," said Horatius, "that you are in a frame of mind to agree to almost anything."

"I am that," said Albert.

"Well, then, my dear fellow," said Horatius, placing his hand affectionately on the other's shoulder, "let me make you an extraordinary proposition. Let me surprise you in turn. I am longing for a change. I have grown rusty here. I need excitement, adventure. A moment ago, as I watched you at work, I could not but reflect upon the attractions of the burglar's calling and wish that I could practice it, if only temporarily, simply for the sake of the sport to be found in it.

"Now, will you not agree to change places with me for a few weeks? You be the cashier — the accounts are simple — I will be the burglar. I will engage to restore your grocery to a sound financial condition in, say two months; and, what is more, I will adopt such a policy as will rid you of the children without arousing the suspicion of the mothers. And the period will be one of huge enjoyment and mental repose for me. What do you say?"

Albert was dumbfounded. "Do you really propose to put a confessed burglar at a cashier's desk?" he asked.

"We agreed that you were only an amateur burglar," Horatius smilingly answered.

"It is a cinch for me. But for you to take up burglary yourself — " said Albert.

"Oh, as you please," Horatius remarked. "I only make the suggestion from a desire for adventure. I had intended going off on a brief vacation to-morrow," he added, reflectively; "but it would be easy for you to explain that I had changed my mind. And, of course, I shall still have the vacation."

"We look so much alike that no one would ever suspect," said Albert. "I assure you the proposal tempts me."

"Close with it," said Horatius, "and I will put on my trousers immediately, and you shall go to bed. Breakfast is at eight. The servant's name is Mary Jane."

"You mean that you will put on *my* trousers?"
said Albert, laughingly. "Here they are!"

With a perfectly grave face Horatius rose, and the
exchange of garments began. In a very few moments
the burglar stood robed in the immaculate night gown

of the cashier, and the cashier had possessed himself of
the burglar's clothes, dark lantern and professional im-
plements. Then the two men clasped hands.

"I assure you I am very much obliged to you,"
said Albert, "and I also assure you I will not betray
your trust."

"I have no fear of that," interposed Horatius, with a slight smile.

"Your action is still perfectly inexplicable to me," Albert went on; "but let us pass that by. I only hope you will enjoy yourself. Of course, it is understood that if you are—hem—tripped up, I continue on as cashier."

"Oh, certainly!"

"Farewell, then. Before you go, you would n't like to tell me what you propose doing with the children, would you?"

Horatius smiled once more. "I will write you a postal card," he said; "and as you will need the combination of the safe, here it is." He took his watch from under his pillow, together with the other valuables he kept there at nights, including the revolver; from the watch case he drew out the slip of paper containing the combination.

"Good-by, Albert," he said.

The next morning, on the arrival of the President, the cashier remarked: "I have decided, sir, that I will not take that vacation."

"Dear me, Mr. Lyman," said the President, in evident surprise; "you did not speak to me of desiring one. But before we go on with the subject, let us count the cash and the securities."

Half an hour later, it had been developed that there was no cash and that the securities had vanished.

and Albert was under arrest. Matters were now clearer to him. That afternoon he received a postal card containing the following words:

"I shall sell toy-pistols."

Thomas Wharton.

A TIMELY HINT.

"She stood with her gracefully
rounded body well set out by the
polished oaken door."

A TIMELY HINT.

GEORGE SCHUYLER went home from the office with two problems on his mind. The first did not worry him much, for it was only a small matter in connection with his business. He was a young architect grappling with his first large order: the erection of a thirteen-story office building.

In one corner of the lot which the structure was to occupy a troublesome bit of quicksand had been discovered; but he knew several ways of overcoming quicksand, and it only remained for him to choose the best of them.

The other question was more important and difficult.

What sort of a Christmas present should he give to a girl who had always had everything she wanted from her cradle up?

He could estimate exactly the tensile strength of any species of building material, or the number of pounds weight that a steel truss would have to sustain; but he knew no formula that would help him in such a case as this.

The trouble seemed to be that while George could

look at the building from a coldly professional standpoint, he could take no such view of anything which
concerned Rose's happiness.

He was not in love with the gi-
gantic mass of brick and iron; but
he was violently, and, so far as he
knew, hopelessly in love with her.

He was willing to give her any
thing that would please her, but
he doubted the good taste of a too
lavish expenditure. No; it must
be some elegant trifle that she had
never seen before, and that would
move her irresistibly to "Love the
Giver." Something that would give her
a hint of the condition of his heart, and prepare her for
the words he hoped to utter, some day.

Rose Wyckoff was the daughter of a man who
valued the substantial fruits of the harvest above the
pink and white buds of the Spring-time.

Most of George's prospects were still in the bud.
When that big building was really finished, and one·or
two more that he hoped to get the orders for under way,
it would be soon enough to approach the old gentleman.

Although George had a very clear idea of what Mr.
Wyckoff would say if he spoke now, he could gain no
idea of what Rose would say; but he was grimly determined to try to be worthy of her. He left the rest
to fate, and contented himself with drawing the designs
for magnificent and glittering castles in Spain.

When George went to call on Rose that evening, he tried to be as cheery and animated as usual, but his nervous and absorbed manner must have given her some hint of the heavy load of anxiety he was carrying; for, as he stood drawing on his overcoat in the hall, after the last good-nights had been said, she threw herself across the outside door, and barred his egress.

As she stood with her gracefully rounded body well set out by the polished oaken door, and her bright face turned up to him with an expression which a bolder man might have almost have construed as an invitation, George felt that he would have given the value of all the buildings that he ever hoped to plan, to tell her how much he thought of her.

He was somewhat surprised at her sudden movement, or as much so as he ever permitted himself to be at any of her actions, which were generally unaccountable from a masculine standpoint. He only thought that if she were going to appear in the character of a jailor, he could stand a life sentence with considerable equanimity.

"Now, before you go, George," said Rose, with her hand still on the knob, "I want to ask you one question. You are not thinking of making a Christmas present to me this year, are you?"

George owned that he had taken the matter into serious consideration.

"And you are determined to persist in doing so in spite of my disapproval?" she asked with a smile that must have warned him that her disapproval would not be of a serious nature, for he had the fine presence of mind to signify firmly that he was not only adamant in that respect but even iridium.

"Well, I like a determined man," admitted Rose, with an admiring glance at his suf-

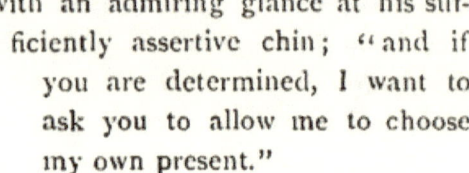

ficiently assertive chin; "and if you are determined, I want to ask you to allow me to choose my own present."

"With pleasure!" exclaimed George.

"That is awfully nice of you," said Rose; "but be sure to remember not to get anything until you hear from me. I will let you know in good time. Must you really go now?" she asked; for George, with the fortuitous absent-mindedness of a truly bashful man, had placed his hand over hers on the knob of the door. "Good-night, then," she said, as it yielded to their united efforts, and George found himself standing outside on the steps. He raised his hat as the door closed gently, as if it were reluctant to shut him out from her presence.

That night George drew some preliminary sketches of the Spanish château, that were full of detail as to the châtelaine, but hazy as to the stairways.

After that, he saw Rose quite often before it was time for the green wreaths to hang in the parlor windows; but she always said that she was not yet ready to tell him what kind of a present she wanted. It was not

until Christmas Eve that he received a little note hastily
scribbled on the back of a visiting card.

Dear George:

*I find that I have neglected to give you the
information I promised. But it does n't matter. We
have gone to the country for our Winter outing, and
Mother wants me to ask you to join us for as many
days as you can spare from business. I hope you
will come and give me a chance to keep my promise.*

Sincerely yours,

Rose.

George accepted this invitation with alacrity. He
put an " Out of Town " sign on his office door, and left
the big building to its own devices.

On New Year's morning, Rose suggested a ride to
Sunset Hill, one of the wildest and most picturesque
spots in the neighborhood; and, after the horses were
brought around to the door, they set out together through

the bright, frosty air. They rode half-way up the hill
and then dismounted and, leaving their horses tied to a
bar-post, followed a rough foot-path to the summit.

Rose stood close to George, looking far out over
the fields and woods and groups of cottages, and gazing
with thoughtful eyes on the Sound, where the snow-
covered ice-cakes glistened in the morning sun.

The strong wind rushed through the trees, and
pressed her closer to him; he steadied her, with very
unsteady hands.

"What a wreck I am!" she said, as she put back
a brown tress which had strayed across her face. "Oh,
I nearly forgot to tell you about my Christmas. Frankly,
would you mind giving a ring to me?"

George's face fell, as he returned; "what kind of a ring? You have so many of them; and I wanted to give you something original."

"A ring would be very original, from *you ;*" and she smiled demurely; "and I fancy a plain turquoise would be the proper thing, now. Here, you may measure my finger; the third, please." And drawing off her glove, she slipped a warm, little left hand into his.

"The third! Why, that is the engagement finger!" exclaimed George, as the air assumed for him the balmy mildness of an Indian Summer.

"You said it yourself, George Schuyler!" she cried, with a brave attempt to be saucy; but her voice was timid and choked, as she rested her delicate head lightly against his shaggy coat; and, now, you can never tell any one I proposed to you, even if—even if this is L— Leap-year."

Harry Romaine.

A BRILLIANT IDEA.

"*Thomas Montgomery Archer*
stands before you."

A BRILLIANT IDEA.

I.

A JOYFUL SMILE lit up Tom Archer's face as he finished the story he was engaged upon, and carefully signed his name in full — *Thomas Montgomery Archer.*

But the smile was followed by a look of despair, as he gazed at the little piles of MSS. scattered here and there about the table — for each little pile was a story or a poem that had been finished a longer or shorter time and was still unpublished.

Tom was an author by profession, but scarcely by practice; except so far as merely writing stories and poems went. His name was but little known to the world, and he was still novice enough to experience a delightful tremor when he saw his name in type. Tom was a martyr — or thought he was — and had lately been comparing himself with the poor authors of Grubb Street, who became famous only after their demise.

This thought came to him as he leaned back and viewed the unfruitful results of his labor.   He reflected that the matter which was before him was sufficient to carry his name down to posterity in case of his sudden death, say by starvation, against which he often fought.

He had come to the city with the firm resolve to win a name for himself.   He had won several names in the past few months, for he had contributed to a society paper a story each week, at the rate of seven dollars per story, and had used a different name each week in order to impress the readers of that periodical with the variety of its writers.

But ere long the paper had ceased to have any readers, and ten days before had succumbed to the inevitable.   So Tom had to struggle as best he could; but it was a struggle against fate.   He was hungry even then, and he had but thirteen cents in his pocket.   He counted it over and reflected that it was an unlucky number.   Then he re-read his latest production, and again smiled approvingly;   after which Melancholy claimed him as her own.

"I 'm afraid to steal, ashamed to beg," he paraphrased, rising from his table and pacing up and down the room; "and as to work — *I won't.*   It 's a shame that Genius can not exist in a city of over a million inhabitants.   If Genius has to go under, why, I 'll go under with it.   I will not degrade the habitation of Genius by causing such habitation to indulge in manual or clerical work.   Jove, I wish I had a good dinner!"

The father of the gods paid no heed to this invocation, and if Archer had expected Ganymede to come through the window with a large plate of ambrosia, he was disappointed. But one disappointment more or less, did not matter — he was used to them.

"I have it!" he suddenly shouted, stopping short in his walk. No messenger of the gods had arrived in any tangible shape, not even a thunderbolt interrupted the miserable mortal. "Fame, fame!" he continued, wildly; "posthumous fame is better than none at all. Genius must have its own reward — aye — Genius *will* conquer! even in death!"

He sat down again at his table — his pen did not travel over the paper with its usual speed; he wrote slowly and thoughtfully. Then he picked up his stories and poems, and enclosed them, each in an envelope, with a short note, and directed them separately to each of the great city dailies. His remaining papers he gathered neatly together — placed a poem entitled, "Why? — A Lament," on the top of the heap and then went out, closing the door with a sigh.

It was nearly six o'clock and Christmas Eve.

The streets were covered with mud and crowded with pedestrians hastening from their labor. Archer pushed through them as best he could, and visited each newspaper office in turn, leaving an envelope of MS. with the small boy who stood guard at the editorial sanctums until every paper had been supplied. Then he ate a supper before a street stand at a cost of four cents, and turned his steps toward the river.

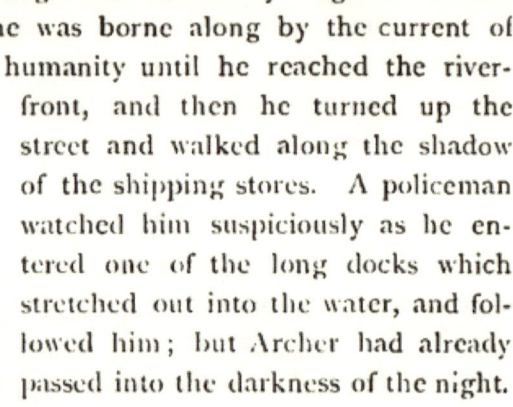

Through the brilliantly lighted streets he was borne along by the current of humanity until he reached the river-front, and then he turned up the street and walked along the shadow of the shipping stores. A policeman watched him suspiciously as he entered one of the long docks which stretched out into the water, and followed him; but Archer had already passed into the darkness of the night.

II.

The editor of *The Echo*, the largest newspaper of the city, came to his post at eight o'clock, and found the MS. and note of poor Tom Archer on his desk. He glanced over it carelessly, and then threw it back on his desk, busying himself with other matter.

About ten o'clock a reporter came in.

"Another poor genius gone," he remarked, as he laid some copy on the desk of the editor. The great man glanced over the item.

"A coat was found by Policeman O'Connell, on Pier 33½ last night. It is supposed that the owner committed suicide, as the policeman had seen a man wandering suspiciously about the dock earlier in the evening, and had ordered him away. The following note was found in the pocket:

Dear J.:

What is the use of living? Genius is not appreciated, and I am hungry, with only thirteen cents wherewith to satisfy my craving.

Thomas Montgomery Archer.

The editor repeated the name.

"Dear me!" he remarked. The item about Tom

fell to the floor. Reaching for the MS. on his desk, the editor read it carefully.

"It has some merit, after all," he said, as he finished it; "I guess I'll put it in the paper with the notice of the poor chap's death, and have Jones write an editorial on it.

> 'Alas! for the rarity,
> Of Christmas Christian charity,' "

he added, as he put a few notes in blue pencil upon the story that Tom Archer had smilingly finished that afternoon.

The readers of the Christmas papers found in each a poem or story by the unfortunate author, accompanied by an account of his suicide and an editorial note on the struggles of Genius in the great metropolis.

III.

That Christmas afternoon the editor of *The Echo* sat in his home, discussing with his son and heir of five years the personality of Santa Claus.

"Excuse me, sir," said a servant at the door; "but there's a man downstairs who wants to see you."

"P'haps it 's Santy," suggested the embryo editor. The real editor smiled — he would foster the belief of his son while he was able.

"Perhaps it is," he said; "ask the gentleman to step in, please." The servant departed. A step was heard outside the door. The son and heir looked expectant and disappointed; for a poor specimen of humanity, unshaven and cold, entered.

"I beg your pardon, sir," said the poor specimen, in better tones than such objects are in the habit of using; "I am sorry to disturb you at your home, but I should like a little money on account. Life has its demands, you know," he added, airily.

"On account!" gasped the editor; "on account of what?"

The small boy crept closer to his father. "P'haps it's Santy in disguise, an' he wants some money to get me more pwesents," whispered the hopeful, regardless of the morning's gifts that littered the floor.

"I am the author of 'A Brilliant Idea,' published in to-day's *Echo*. Tom Archer is my name, now—"

"*What!*" cried the editor, leaping to his feet. "Archer jumped off of a dock last night. Do you take me for a fool?"

"Really, I never gave it much thought," responded Archer, haughtily; "but I am prepared to argue the question with you if you repeat your previous assertion. I can assure you that Archer is no idiot, however; and to prove my statement, he offers to write you up the exclusive account of the results of 'A Brilliant Idea.'

"'A Voice from the Dead,' how would that do for a head-line? The papers to-day are full of my praise — just think of the 'beat' you will have on them. Thomas Montgomery Archer stands before you with a wonderful proposition. After writing the article I have indicated, he would be pleased to be attached to the staff of *The Echo*. At the present moment, though," added the embodiment of Genius, "he seeks the staff of life."

The editor thought a moment. "You would be valuable in emergencies," he said, laughing; "I'll take

your offer.   Come with me and tell me your trials while
you eat."

*   ◂   *   ❋   ✱

"But to whom did you address your note?" asked
the editor, as Archer folded his napkin, satisfied and
contented. "You say that you have no friends."

"To Jove," said Tom, accepting with a smile the
cigar offered him.   "I usually invoke the old gentleman, but this is the first time he ever responded. Possibly he was touched by my addressing him as 'Dear J.'"

Flavel Scott Mines.

THE MAN WITH THE BLACK CRAPE MASK.

13

*"Burying his face in his hands,
he said: 'Give me the mask!'"*

THE MAN WITH THE BLACK CRAPE MASK.

IT WAS on the whitest kind of a white Winter morning that Silas Drummond made his first appearance on the main thoroughfare of Scuttle Hole. He was a tall, angular man, with a military bearing, whose dignity only served to draw attention to his most conspicuous feature. This feature consisted of a jet-black mask, or false face, which fitted him so closely and perfectly that at a short distance it gave him the appearance of a negro. But upon meeting him face to face, it was plain to the observer that he wore a mask of crape. Although he attracted the attention of every one, he did n't seem in the least disconcerted by the open-mouthed wonder that he caused.

Children would watch him as he approached, only to fly, as though pursued by an evil spirit, before he was within a hundred feet of them. Women driving along the road would watch him as he passed, and seldom failed to follow him with their eyes until he had completely vanished. Although the black crape mask made Silas Drummond the most talked-of man from

one end of Scuttle Hole to the other, it had not the
effect of ruffling the serenity of his spirit in the least.

He lived in his own simple way, without a companion, in a little cabin, unpainted, and almost as black as
his crape mask, just below the little graveyard on the
outskirts of the town.

Many were the speculations of the gossips of Scuttle
Hole to account for Mr. Drummond and his weird ec-
centricity. There was an almost uncanny fascination
about it, that grew day by day.

Some thought that the black crape mask could be
worn only by a criminal, in short, a fugitive from justice.
Others argued more charitably that it might have me-
dicinal properties, such, for instance, as would make it
a blessing to any neuralgic sufferer. At any rate, the
mystery remained unsolved, no one caring to presume

on a nodding acquaintance to ask Mr. Drummond for
an explanation of what they considered, after all, was
a matter that concerned none so much as himself.

When Mr. Drummond walked through the streets,
he held his head in the air, as if he were proud of his
black crape mask. It was noticed by all who came in
contact with him that the mask fitted every feature as
though it had been made from a mould of his face.
Upon each side of it there was an aperture that en-
circled the ear, and held the mask firmly in place, so
that there was no chance of its ever falling, and expos-
ing the features of Mr. Drummond to the public eye.

Many conjectures were made relative to his connec-
tions, and many believed firmly that the man with the
black crape mask was not of sound mind; and the
longer he lingered in Scuttle Hole, the greater the mystery became. He was more than a nine-day's wonder,
and interest in him never abated. He was never seen
in church, or, in fact, at any other public gathering,
and no one had more than the slightest acquaintance
with him. But at every store, where two or three were
gathered together, he was the unvarying topic of conversation. Folk wondered how long he had been wearing the crape mask, and how long he would continue
to wear it, and if he kept it on at night when he went
to bed.

Finally, the people of Scuttle Hole began to feel
that the presence of Silas Drummond, with his black
crape mask, was exerting an uncanny influence over them
that it was impossible to shake off; and a deputation of

prominent citizens waited upon the Rev. Eliphalet White
to ask him to call upon Mr. Drummond, and to get from
him, if possible, an explanation of his very strange be-
havior.   The reverend gentleman was not over-pleased
at the commission he was called upon to execute; but

in response to a demand which appeared to be so
general, he consented, fully believing in his heart that
the welfare of the community was at stake.

He started for Mr. Drummond's weather-beaten
abode near the lonely graveyard late on the afternoon of
a stormy Winter day.   It was snowing quite hard, and
the wind seemed to be blowing in every direction.   As
the Reverend EliphaletWhite stood before the cedar-
dotted graveyard, through which the snow was whirling
in mad eddies that seemed to his excited imagination
like the ghosts of those worthies buried below whirling
in a wild waltz to the weird fantastic music of the wind,
he did not feel in the most cheerful frame of mind.

He thrust his chin as far down between the points of his great-coat collar as possible, and, looking toward the ground, hurried on. It was but a few steps to Mr. Drummond's abode, and he was soon at the gate. There was but one light in the house, a candle with a fitful, uneven flame that made an effect anything but pleasant. There was a smouldering log on the hearth that brightened up a bit when a gust of wind came down the chimney. The room was almost dark, but still the clergyman could see, beside the fire, a pair of white hands clasped in the darkness. At first they were as perfectly still as though they had been carved marble, then they began to move, the fingers of one hand drumming upon the knuckles of the other. Then the hands separated, and became invisible.

The clergyman was almost too frightened to knock on the door, until the log blazed up, and he discerned that the hands, in becoming invisible, had been simply thrust into the pockets of the owner, Silas Drummond. The blazing log showed him brooding in silence, as he looked into the embers through the eye-holes in his black crape mask.

"If only to break the awful spell, I will knock," said the trembling clergyman.

When he had done so, Silas Drummond arose suddenly, and, opening the door, bade him enter and be seated. The Reverend Eliphalet White did not feel at all at ease as he accepted the proffered chair. The wind was moaning without, and the windows rattled, and he remembered the flying snow dancing like ghosts in the lonely graveyard, and here he was, sitting opposite the man with the black crape mask.

"I trust, sir," began the clergyman, "that you will pardon me for this intrusion. And I trust that you may appreciate the delicate nature of my errand, which, I can assure you, is a very unpleasant one."

He could see two eyes glisten through the holes in the crape mask during a painful silence of some seconds.

"I have been sent by many worthy members of my congregation to pray that you will give me an explanation of your habit of wearing a crape mask."

The clergyman felt greatly relieved when he had thus delivered himself.

"I am a singularly unfortunate man," replied Mr. Drummond. "I have a mental peculiarity — I call it a mental peculiarity simply for want of a better name — that is possessed by no other man on earth. I have no inner conscience. If I may so put it, I am all outer conscience; and my great misfortune lies in the fact that instead of thinking within, I think without, so that my thoughts, being visible on my face, may be readily read by any one who chances to meet me. For this reason I always wear a mask, and keep away from my fellow-men, until I know that my thoughts are of such a character as to bear the most critical scrutiny. If I shake hands with any man, I will thereafter think within, while he will think without, as I do now. And he will think without until he shakes hands with another, when the latter will be afflicted as I am now. I don't think you would dare to shake hands with me," said Mr. Drummond.

"What! I would n't dare to shake your hand!" replied the Reverend Eliphalet White, feeling all the virtuous strength of his good life tingling in his finger-tips.

"There!"

He extended his hand, and Mr. Drummond took it.

"Now look in the glass."

The clergyman did so for a moment, and burying his face in his hands, said:

"Give me the mask!"

Mr. Drummond removed the black crape mask for the first time, and handed it to the clergyman.

When he returned that night to his own fireside, many of his parishioners were on hand awaiting his arrival in great suspense, to ascertain the result of his mission. When he entered the room with the black crape mask on his face, there was a great commotion. Although his face was not visible, he acted in the same mysterious way that had characterized Mr. Drummond. He seemed filled with a dreadful boding. His wife almost fainted, as she asked for the explanation of the horrible fascination of the black crape mask.

"Ah, would that I dare take it off," he said.

He then made an explanation of his visit.

"I will shake your hand," said Deacon Briggs, one of the most highly esteemed men in Scuttle Hole.

"I would rather not, Deacon," replied the clergyman. "I think I need the black crape mask for some time to come."

But the Deacon, either out of what he considered a kindness to the clergyman, or to show the confidence he felt in the purity of his thoughts, grasped the hand of the latest owner of the black crape mask, and when he looked in the glass at the end of the room, he held his handkerchief over his features until he could hide his countenance behind the welcome shadow of the black crape mask.

In a short time the mask changed faces so many times that no one could be found who cared to shake hands with its owner, for the fear of having to ask for it.

For the many, many years that the black crape mask remained the wonder of Scuttle Hole, it covered the features of this man. It then became a belief that amounted to a superstition that no man could possess it, without using it as a screen for the thoughts that burned upon his features. But this, at least, proved to be fallacious. The impossible is always coming to pass.

The black crape mask has found at last an owner whose thoughts are of so pure and chaste a character, that they would bear the sharpest scrutiny of the severest moral critic. He lives in a halo of the people's love; he is the idol and the model of all who glory in walking

the straight and narrow path; he is at once the joy
and the envy of the Rev. Eliphalet White; he is the
man whose mind is never sullied by an impure thought.
He is, in short, Dominick Funshon, Scuttle Hole's practical plumber.

R. K. Munkittrick.

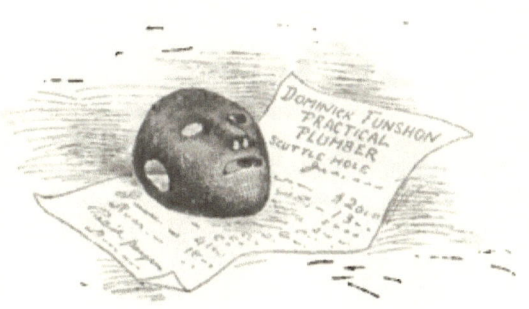

THE RECORDING SPOOK.

"'Sweets to the sweet'," he would say. "That's what you said to her when you gave her the rose."

THE RECORDING SPOOK.

IT MAY BE that the brief statement which I have to
make is to some extent out of place, coming from
me, a mere layman. I have felt, indeed, that it ought
to be left to a scientific man. But I think that, even in
the incomplete manner in which I must present it, it
may have a certain intrinsic interest for those who have
given any thought to the great problem of what we
know as the supernatural. The period which allows of
the existence of a Society for Psychical Research — the
period which pries curiously into our personal relations
with the unseen world — must plead my excuse for offering you my small contribution to the science of the
unknowable.

The incidents which I am about to narrate occurred
some two years ago. It was toward the close of an
exhausting season. I had striven for some months to
perform that part known as "keeping one's end up."
I had tried to keep my end up. There is concurrent
and contemporaneous testimony to the effect that I did
keep my end up. Looking back on it now, it seems to
me that I kept two or three ends up. I kept my end up

at afternoon teas.   I kept my end up at early morning
suppers.   I was up before, and after, the lark.   I generally managed to see the moon to bed.   I do not know
whether I make this clear to you.   As I said, perhaps I
ought to have left the subject to a scientific man.   Any
scientific man could explain that this sort of a thing is
wearing on the most cast-iron constitution.

One dewy morn in February, I slipped into bed
just as the first milk cart rattled under my window.   I

was very tired.   I was very tired, indeed.   My eyes were
just closing when I saw, seated upon the foot of my
bed, what I can only describe as a supernatural visitant.

It was a pale-gray, mottled spook, about sixteen
hands high.   I was n't afraid of it.   I said:

"Hello! who are you?"

"I 'm a spook," it replied.

"All right," I said; "spook when you 're spooken
to.   Good night."   And then I turned over.

"Where are you going?" inquired the spook.

"Going to sleep," I told him.

"Not now, you're not," said the spook.

"What's to hinder me?" I queried, in a scientific spirit.

"I am," the spook said; "that's what I'm here for. I'm the recording spook. I'm sent here to wait on you every night, when you go to bed, and to report to you, before you go to sleep, every foolish, conventional or unnecessary thing that you have said during the day."

I mildly intimated that he had a large contract on hand.

"I have," said he, rubbing his hands; "and I'm the boy that can fill it, too. Come now, young man, roll over so that I can see you, take your hands out of your ears and listen. The entertainment is going to begin right now, and the curtain's up."

I groaned. I might as well have whistled.

"Let's see," said the spook, grinning hideously and rubbing his hands; "let's see. You met Jones at the Club this morning. You had n't seen Jones in two days, and what did you say to Jones? Why, you said: 'Quite a stranger, are n't you?' Now, that was brilliant, was n't it? The edge had n't been rubbed off that observation

14

in fifteen hundred third-class boarding-houses, had it?
Why, that was the regulation joke in the ark when
Noah happened to miss a breakfast through sitting up
too late the night before inspecting his private stock.

"Go away," said I.   "I want to go to sleep."

But he did n't go away.   He went — he
went on :

"Then you went to the Turkish
bath, did n't you?   And you went into
the hot room — temperature 200.   And
you saw Robinson there, eh?   And what
did you say to Robinson ? "

I said that I did n't remember.

"You *do* remember," said the spook; "you said:
'Is it hot enough for you?'—that 's what you said.
You did n't happen to think of any other way of making
an idiot of yourself, just at the moment, so you said
that.   Well, it filled the bill."

That is the way he began, that spook; and he
kept it up until daylight.   He did n't seem to get tired,
either.   He just kept it up, talking away in that easy,
pleasant, conversational manner, telling me all the idiotic
things I had said that day.   I rolled about, and tried
to bury my ears in the pillows.   Then I tried to bury
the pillows in my ears.   It was of no use.   The experience meeting came to a close about half-past six.   The
spook vanished, after making an appointment for the
next morning.

He was on time; he was on time right straight
along every night after that.   I never went to sleep until

I knew just how much of a conversational ass I had made of myself during the preceding twenty-four hours.

Under these kindly ministrations I improved in my speech. I chastened my conversation, and turned the faucet on my flow of language. And I saw with pleasure that the spook began to dwindle and diminish and grow pale and peaky. He got in a ten or fifteen minutes' séance each night, to remind me that I had said "See you later," or "I should smile," or something of that sort, for I found it difficult to get rid of the slang habit. But he dwindled — every blessèd night he dwindled.

But one night I came home and found that spook swollen to twice his original proportions. His head was bobbing up against the ceiling, and there was a grin of fiendish malice on his face.

I knew what was the matter. I knew he had me, too. That evening I had met, for the first time, a certain young lady, and I felt — as one does sometimes feel in such cases — without any arguing about it, or making any investigation into the subject, that without her my life would be a barren blank, not to speak about a desert waste. I suppose that is what is called falling in love. Well, that is what I called it, a little later.

But it was a great thing for the spook. He fairly battened on me from that time on.

"'Sweets to the sweet,'" he would say. "That 's what you said to her when you gave her the rose. Why, the girl must think you a perfect imbecile!"

"She does n't," I would explain. "She told a friend of mine that I was a brilliant conversationalist."

"Oh, you 're a brilliant conversationalist!" he would shriek; "and did the brilliant conversationalist brill this evening? Not this evening. The brilliant conversationalist asked her if she did n't think the rooms were very warm. And he said that we had been having very pleasant weather for this time of year, and that it would probably be warmer in May. Oh, you just bristled all over with pungent epigrams, you did!"

I did n't care, though. I have no use for a man who can be in love and not make a fool of himself. And I was happy.

And the end came. There was one night when I got home, and found the spook swelled to such proportions that he filled the apartments. I had to walk through him to get to bed. His gray, mottled sides shook with hysterical laughter. There was malicious

triumph in his distended eyes.   He pointed his finger
at me, and gasped out: "Oh, what a fool you've made
of yourself this evening!   Oh, ain't I going to have fun
with you!"

He never had it.   His memory had got an overdose
of conversational idiocy, and his surcharged brain gave
way under the strain.   He gurgled and burbled for a
little, and tried to tell me all about it; but it was too
much for him; and at last, with one wild howl of im-
becility, he vanished utterly away.

That, I should explain, was the evening that I asked
the young lady to be my wife.   And it was also the
evening when the young lady said: "Why — yes."

And what I said after that was too much for the
spook.

H. C. Bunner.